DUSTY LEADS THE CHARGE...

As the dying horse crumpled, he sprang from its back. His momentum carried him clear, but he was in danger of being ridden down by the rushing men behind him.

Looking back, he saw a riderless horse approaching in the lead of the Company. Twirling away the revolver, he sprang forward to catch hold of the empty saddle's horn and vaulted astride. The leather was slick with the previous user's blood, but he retained his seat and charged onwards. Without any conscious thought on his part, he drew the revolver ready for use.

Springing away from the half-turned gun, the sergeant chief-of-piece rushed at Dusty and lashed out with his short artillery sword. Down flicked the small Texan's Haiman sabre, catching and deflecting the Yankee's blade. Then Dusty lunged, driving his point into the man's chest and dragging it free as the horse carried him by...

J.T. Edson

KILL DUSTY FOG!

CHARTER BOOKS, NEW YORK

This Charter book contains the complete
text of the original edition.
It has been completely reset in a typeface
designed for easy reading and was printed
from new film.

KILL DUSTY FOG!

A Charter Book / published by arrangement with
Transworld Publishers, Ltd.

PRINTING HISTORY
Corgi edition published 1970
Charter edition / July 1987

ISBN: 0-441-44110-6

Charter Books are published by The Berkley Publishing Group,
200 Madison Avenue, New York, NY 10016.
PRINTED IN THE UNITED STATES OF AMERICA

As the world is divided into two parts, Great Britain and its colonies, I dedicate this book to Mike Prorok of Chicago, the Colonial Gentleman.

CHAPTER ONE

This's Real Helpful of the Yankees

The attack came suddenly, unexpectedly and with devastating effectiveness. Certainly the idea that it might happen had never entered 1st Lieutenant Savos' head as he rode along the narrow woodland trail leading to Little Rock, followed by the two lumbering 10-inch siege mortar-wagons and their caisson which formed his platoon.

Earlier that morning his platoon, last in the battery's line of march, had been forced to halt when the near rear wheel of the leading mortar-wagon showed signs of slipping from its axle. On being informed of the mishap, the battery's commanding officer had ordered that Savos' men must correct the fault themselves and follow as quickly as possible. Due to a delay in the arrival of a courier, there had been little enough time for the battery to assemble, load their heavy mortars and march to Little Rock where they were ordered to be present for inspection by the newly arrived General Horace Trumpeter.

So Savos and his men had been compelled to deal with the matter unaided. He suspected that his two "chief-of-piece" sergeants had conspired to delay the work, ensuring that they would arrive too late to join the ranks of artillery, infantry, cavalry and shiny-butts from the various non-combatant Departments, which even at that moment would be forming up on the open ground at the edge of the town. Neither sergeant had troubled to hide his objections to being uprooted from their comfortable camp as part of the garrison at Hot Springs just to welcome General Trumpeter. He was the latest in a line of Generals sent to lead the Union's Army of Arkansas to ascendancy over the Rebs

1

who held the land south and west of the Ouachita. Or to
try; for the predominantly Texas regiments of Ole Devil
Hardin, commanding general of the Confederate States'
Army of Arkansas, showed a marked strenuous reluctance
to being ascended.

"Can't we make any better speed than this, Sergeant
Cragg?" Savos asked petulantly, looking back as he started
to ride beneath the spreading branches of a large old white
oak that grew at the side of the trail.

"*We* can," Cragg answered, not leaving his place by the
near lead horse. "It's the hosses 'n' wagon's slow us
dow—"

Before the reply ended, the sergeant saw something
which drove it out of his mind. Unfortunately, his realization of the sight's implications came a shade too late.

A shape launched itself from amongst the thick foilage
of the white oak. Hurling down from the lowest branch, it
caught Savos by the shoulders and dragged him from his
saddle.

With a feeling of shock, Cragg realized that, although
bareheaded, the attacker from the oak tree wore the uniform of a Confederate cavalry officer. There were other
significant factors which might have occurred to him,
given time; but, even as the realization came, he found
himself with troubles of his own. Something hissed
through the air. Coming from among bushes at the side of
the trail, the running noose of a rope fell over his head and
tightened about his shoulders. Feeling himself being hauled
from his horse, he let out a startled yell. He forgot about
his officer's predicament and gave his attention to saving
himself. Even as he kicked his feet free from the stirrup
irons and concentrated on attempting to hit the ground
standing up, he saw that he could expect little immediate
assistance from his companions.

Unlike members of "field" artillery batteries, the siege-
mortar crews did not ride on the team horses or wagons.
Instead, with the exception of the officer and chiefs-of-
piece, they marched alongside the heavy draught horses
which pulled their weapons. Dressed for the review, they

had their short artillery swords slung on their belts. The swords proved to be woefully inadequate.

Men clad in uniforms of cadet-grey, tight-legged breeches with yellow cavalry stripes down the outer seams and knee-high riding boots, appeared on either side of the trail. Some rose from among the bushes, or dropped off over-hanging branches while others sprang from behind tree trunks.

Unnoticed by the Yankee artillery-men, a rope slanted upwards from the lower limbs of a chestnut tree into those of the big old oak opposite. Leaves rustled where the rope disappeared at its lower end. Gripping it, a tall, wide-shouldered young 1st lieutenant swung out of the foliage. Hatless, he had a thatch of rumpled, fiery hair and a cheery, pugnaciously handsome face. Around his waist, hanging lower than the usual military pattern, was a weapon belt carrying two walnut handled 1860 Army Colts butt-forward in open-topped holsters. Not that he attempted to draw the revolvers. His open legs wrapped around the torso of the open-mouthed, staring second chief-of-piece and the force of his arrival bore the other from his saddle. Dumping the sergeant to the ground, the Rebel lieutenant dropped to land astride him. Around lashed the officer's fist, colliding hard against the noncon's jaw. Going limp, the victim slid limply to his assailant's feet.

Bursting on to the trail without allowing the rope between them to slacken, Cragg's captor proved to be a gangling Confederate sergeant major with a prominent adam's apple and a worried, care-worn face. Despite his melancholy appearance, the sergeant major acted with speed and efficiency. Under the propulsion of his hands, the hard-plaited Manila rope seemed to take life. Two coils rolled forward, dropping one after the other over Cragg's shoulders and further pinioning his arms. Wild with anger, but unable to free himself, he attempted a kick at the approaching Rebel. Down stabbed the miserable Rebel's left hand. Deftly he caught Cragg's rising foot. With a jerk and twist, the sergeant major tumbled the Yankee face down. Before the chief-of-piece could recover his breath, his cap-

tor had secured his ankles and completed the job by drawing and lashing his wrists together.

More by luck than riding skill, Savos managed to quit
his saddle and land on his feet. Spitting out startled oaths,
he thrust his assailant away. In a quick glance around, he
learned the full extent of the danger. None of his men carried firearms and all looked to be proving too slow at
drawing their swords. Their attackers, on the other hand,
held Army Colts, although apparently contenting themselves with taking prisoners, for there was no shooting.
From studying the situation, Savos jerked his head around
and stared at the figure whose dramatic appearance had
sparked off the assault.

Five foot six at most in height, Savos' attacker looked
very young. More so when the triple three-inch-long, half-
inch-wide gold bars on his stand-up collar and double braid
yellow silk "chicken-guts" up the outside of his tunic's
sleeves announced him to be a captain in the Confederate
States Army. He had curly, dusty blond hair and was handsome, although not in an eye-catching manner. Savos read
a strength and power in the young face that matched the
width of the shoulders and slim-waisted development of his
small frame. The tunic ended at waist level, without the
"skirt extending half-way between hip and knee" as required by the C.S.A.'s *Manual of Dress Regulations*. A
tight-rolled, scarlet silk bandana replaced the black cravat
of a formal uniform, its ends trailing over the tunic. While
his trousers and boots conformed to *Dress Regulations,* he
wore a non-issue gunbelt similar to that of the red-haired
lieutenant. In its holsters carefully designed and cut to their
fit, two bone-handled Army Colts pointed their butts to the
front.

All that Savos saw as he spluttered another curse and
started to bring up his fists. Clearly the Rebels did not
intend to risk the sound of shots reaching Union ears. In
which case, Savos figured that he stood a chance. Having
boxed in his Eastern college, he expected no difficulty in
felling his small attacker. With the captain in his hands, he
could compel the other Rebels to surrender. Rumour had it

that they showed more loyalty to their officers than did members of the Union Army, a thing he could turn to his advantage.

However Savos was given no opportunity to put his skill as a pugilist into use. Already the small Rebel was moving closer. Gliding forward, he struck at the lieutenant with lightning speed. The way in which he held his hand, with fingers extended together and thumb bent over the up-turned palm, looked amateurish to one trained in the noble art of pugilism. Yet he had no cause for complaint about the result of the blow. Referring to the impact against his solar plexus in later years, Savos would liken it to being kicked with the sharp hoof of a wounded bull wapiti, or running full-tilt into a sword's blunted point. Such fanciful descriptions did not occur to him at the moment of receipt. With a strangled croak, he doubled over and fell back a couple of steps.

Following Savos up, the captain struck again. Still he did not clench his fist, but chopped the heel of his open hand against the side of the other's neck. Once more the awkward method in no way impaired the efficiency of the attack. On the arrival of the blow, Savos collapsed in a limp pile on the trail.

Clearly, the captain did not doubt that his methods would produce the desired effect, for he turned his attention to what was going on about him immediately after striking Savos the second time. A faint grin twisted at his lips as he watched the red haired lieutenant fell the sergeant and spring clear. Turning with his fists raised, the red head glared around as if hoping for a chance to use them. However such had been the speed and surprise of the attack that he found no takers. Already the Yankee artillerymen were standing with raised hands, looking into the muzzles of persuasive revolvers.

After studying the wagons, the captain looked along the trail. He saw that the horses of Savos and the two Yankee sergeants had been caught by the men positioned earlier for that duty. Satisfied that the horses could not give warning by running riderless across the rolling, open land beyond the woods, he turned back to his men. He walked across to where his mournful-featured sergeant major stood with an expression so worried that he and not the Yankees might have been captured.

"Did any of them get away, Billy Jack?" the captain asked, his voice a pleasant Texas drawl.

"Nary a one," the sergeant major replied miserably.

"All right your side, Cousin Red?" the captain went on.

"We got 'em all, Cousin Dusty," the red headed lieutenant answered.

"Have them hawg-tied," ordered the captain. "I'll go make sure that Yankee luff's* not hurt bad. It's easy to hit just a mite too hard when you use the *tegatana* against the side of the neck."

Despite his concern, the captain found Savos groaning his way slowly to consciousness. Relieving the lieutenant of his revolver and sword—the officer alone wearing a firearm on his belt—the young Rebel stood back with an air of satisfaction. Hooves sounded and he turned to face a tall red-haired soldier who was approaching, leading three horses and carrying the company's guidon. Spiking the end of the guidon's pole into the ground, the soldier allowed the horses' long, split-end reins to dangle free. Going to the big black stallion on the right of the trio, he took the white Jeff Davis campaign hat from where it hung by its storm strap on the low horned, double girthed saddle.

"Figured you'd need this, Cap'n Dusty," the guidon carrier remarked, offering the hat to the small blond.

Shaking his head, fingering the side of his neck and groaning, Savos forced himself into a sitting position. Slowly the mists swirled away from before his eyes and he took in the scene around him. Not far away, the small captain stood donning the campaign hat. On its front was a silver badge formed of a five-pointed star in a circle. That meant he was a member of the Texas Light Cavalry. The saddles of the three exceptional fine horses, each carrying a sabre and coiled rope on opposing sides of its low horn, gave added confirmation of the regiment to which the

---

* Luff: derogatory name for a young 1st lieutenant.

Rebels belonged, the double girths being peculiar to the Lone Star State.

Looking next towards his halted mortar-wagons, Savos saw his men being disarmed or tied up hand and foot. As he swung angrily toward the captain, intending to protest about such treatment, a puff of wind fluttered the Rebel company's guidon and drew his attention to it. The sight of the letter it carried momentarily drove all thoughts of objecting out of his head.

From studying the letter "C" on the guidon, Savos jerked his head around and stared at the small captain. The man who commanded Company "C" of the Texas Light Cavalry had a name well-known on the Arkansas battle-front. Yet could that short, almost insignificant-looking captain, not more than eighteen years of age and a young eighteen at that, be the famous Dusty Fog?

Over the past year, Captain Dusty Fog of the Texas Light Cavalry had become much mentioned by virtue of his excellence as a military raider. In fact, many men who had been matched against him ranked the leader of Company "C" with those two other Dixie masters, Turner Ashby and John Singleton Mosby. The Texans fighting to retain the Toothpick State for the South held Dusty Fog in higher esteem than Ashby or even than the "Grey Ghost," Mosby himself.

Nephew of Ole Devil Hardin, Dusty Fog was a native Texan. So the other sons of the Lone Star State accorded him pride of place. They boasted of his lightning fast draw and deadly revolver-shooting skill, or told tales about his uncanny ability at barehanded fighting. There were few, however, who could have told from whom he had learned his peculiar, yet effective skills in the latter. The truth was that he had been taught the secrets—all but unknown in the Western Hemisphere at that time—of *ju-jitsu* and *karate* by Old Devil Hardin's Japanese servant, using them to back up his not inconsiderable strength and to off-set his lack of inches.

To the Union soldiers on the eastern side of the Ouachita River, Dusty Fog's name had become synonymous with trouble, misery and disaster. At the head of the hard-riding, harder-fighting Company "C," he played havoc with the Yankees in Arkansas. He struck when least expected, with the raging fury of a Texas twister and left destruction as great as any claused by a whirlwind in his wake. For all that, many Union soldiers regarded him with open, or grudging, admiration. He was recognized by the majority of them as a courageous, resourceful, yet chivalrous enemy.

Among his other exploits had been the destruction of a vitally important bridge over the Moshogen River. In a way that particular raid could be blamed for Savos' present misfortune. Learning that a Yankee lieutenant was falsely accused of cowardice and desertion for his conduct during the attack on the bridge, Dusty Fog had offered to attend the officer's court martial to give evidence. This had been arranged by Old Devil Hardin, through the Union Amry's top brass. Although he had travelled under a flag of truce, Dusty was compelled on three occasions to defend his life; culminating with his killing General Buller in a duel which the other—who had personal reasons for wanting the lieutenant convicted—had forced upon him.* Buller's death had created a vacancy in Arkansas which Trumpeter had filled and so, indirectly, had caused Savos to leave the safety of the Hot Springs' defences and fall into the Rebels' hands.

After putting on his hat, the small Texan walked towards Savos. There was none of the cocky swagger which might have been expected from one so young and small who held a rank of some importance. Savos became aware of the strength of the other's personality. That was no mere stripling half-pint holding rank because of kin-ship with important Rebels and controlling his men through family influence or the *Manual of Field Regulations*. Much to his annoyance, Savos found himself sitting up straighter as he would when approached by a senior officer of his own regiment.

"Are you all right, mister?" the captain asked.

* Told in *The Fastest Gun in Texas*.

"Yes—sir," Savos answered, the honorific popping out of his mouth before he could prevent it. "Are you Dusty Fog?"

"Captain Dustine Edward Marsden Fog," confirmed the small Texan. "None of your men are seriously injured. I'll be leaving you hawg-tied and under guard for a spell, mister; but I'll make sure that one of you can get loose afore we pull out."

"What're you going to do?" Savos inquired, understanding the reason why his men were being tied.

"I'm figuring on firing a salute for your new general," Dusty drawled. "And I don't want you around trying to spoil it."

"You—you mean that you're go—?" Savos croaked, staring him disbelief at the two squat mortars. Then he turned his eyes to the caisson, knowing what it held.

"Just that," Dusty confirmed and nodded to where the red-haired lieutenant was approaching. "Mr. Blaze here'll look to you, but don't try anything *loco,* mister."

"*Loco* being Spanish for crazy, friend," drawled 1st Lieutenant Charles William Henry Blaze cheerfully. "Which trying to escape, or make fuss for us'd be."

First Lieutenant Blaze might have been baptized Charles William Henry, but it was doubtful if even he remembered the fact. His thatch of fiery, ever-untidy hair had qualified him for his commonly-used name "Red". Dressed in a similar regulation-flouting uniform to his cousin, it carried two collar bars and a single-braid "chicken guts" insignia.

Already Red Blaze had built up a reputation for courage, possessing a hot temper and an almost unequalled ability to become involved in fights. Yet Dusty recognized that he had virtues which more than off-set his minor faults, including one which few people noticed. Older senior officers tended to think of Red as irresponsible, but Dusty knew better. Given a job to do, Red became calm and let nothing distract him. Aware of that, Dusty never hesitated to trust Red to carry out any duty he was given.

Leaving his cousin to deal with Savos, Dusty walked over to join his lean sergeant major. As always Billy Jack

looked a picture of dejection. The peaked forage cap had
never been regarded as a thing of beauty and the one
perched on Billy Jack's head increased his general lugu-
brious appearance. There was nothing smart about his uniform, the three stripes and arc of silk announcing his rank
coming almost as a surprise. Yet he was real good with the
two Army Colts hanging in the open-topped holsters low
on his thighs. Maybe Billy Jack conveyed the impression
of always expecting the worst, but Dusty knew him to be a
tough, shrewd fighting man and well deserving of his rank.

"We done got these-here stove-pipes, Cap'n Dusty,"
Billy Jack announced miserably, nodding towards the
mortar-wagons. "Now I surely hope you ain't thinking of
trying what I know you're thinking of trying with 'em."

"We are," Dusty assured him. "Why else did I have you
boys learning how to use artillery the last time Uncle Devil
took us off patrols to rest up the horses?"

"Just being your usual ornery self," the sergeant major
answered *sotto voce,* then grinned with all the insincerity
of a professional politician meeting a rival for office, and
went on in a louder tone, "I allus figured you'd got a right
good reason for doing it."

"And I heard you the first time," Dusty warned him.
"Damned if I wouldn't bust you to private, but the rest of
this bunch're worse than you. Anyways, let's take a look at
what we've got. Way that Yankee luff jumped when I said
we're fixing to fire a salute for Trumpeter, he's toting along
everything we'll need to do it."

"That's what I figured you aimed to do," Billy Jack
wailed. "It's all your fault he's here, anyways."

"How come?" Dusty asked, as they walked to the first
wagon.

"If you-all hadn't downed that nice ole General Buller,
in a duel, for shame, they wouldn't've had to replace him.
Now they've done sent along a regular fire-eating, ring-
tailer ripper who allows he'll have all us poor lil' Texas
boys drove back across the Red River in a month and'll be
eating supper at the Governor's mansion in Houston comes
early fall."

Knowing just how much the other's woe-filled tirade meant, Dusty ignored it. For a moment he studied the mortar on the leading wagon, then nodded his head approvingly. Just as he had expected, the weapon was of the same pattern as those used by the Confederate States' Army. So he and his men could set it up, load and fire it with no great difficulty. Whether they could operate the mortars to the best of their potential was another matter. Dusty hoped that they could.

Sent to meet a Confederate agent and collect his information, Dusty had learned of the grand review in Trumpeter's honour. At the first there had seemed to be nothing he and his Company could hope to achieve against the large number of troops who had been assembled. He had ridden in the direction of Little Rock with no greater intention than to learn if Trumpeter had brought fresh regiments, or new, improved weapons along. When his forward scout had brought word of the unescorted mortar platoon, Dusty had seen a chance of intervening. So he had arranged and sprung the trap into which Savos marched so blindly. Even if he could not make use of the mortars, destroying them noisily near Little Rock would serve to show how little the C.S.A. in general and the Texas Light Cavalry in particular feared Trumpeter's threats of driving them back into Texas and capturing the capital city of Houston.

While the capture of the battery had been accomplished easily, using the mortars would still be anything but a sinecure. A month's training with the artillery had taught him the basic principles involved in firing different weapons. But there was much he did not know, particularly about the correct fusing of the mortar shells.

Yet the temptation to make a more dramatic gesture than merely blowing up the mortars was great. Not for Dusty's personal aggrandizement, he cared nothing about that, but as a means of lowering the Yankee's morale. If it could be done—

Letting the thought hang in the air, Dusty went by the second wagon. He climbed on to the caisson and raised the lid of the first chest. Inside lay everything he would need:

the round shells, powder charges made up in serge bags, boxes of fuses, lanyards, friction primers. The caisson also carried handspikes, rammers loading tongs and sponge-buckets, all of which his men knew how to use. Most important, to Dusty's way of thinking, was a sheet of paper fastened to the inside of the chest's lid.

"Well now," the small Texan said, reading the printed instructions listing angles for firing at various ranges and times of the shell's flight at those distances. "This's *real* helpful of the Yankees."

"It sure is," agreed Billy Jack dolefully. "Now we'll know what we've done wrong when we get blowed up."

Which, as Dusty knew, was unqualified support for his scheme. Given that much information, they could use the mortars with reasonable efficiency. Certainly sufficiently well for his purposes. So he grinned at his sergeant major and said, "All right, let's go show our respects to the general."

CHAPTER TWO

You Sure Ruined His Review

"The review's formed up to the north of town and well clear of it," Red Blaze reported with satisfaction as he rejoined his cousin on the edge of the woodland in which they had captured the Yankee mortar platoon. "There're none of our folks watching that I could see."

After securing the prisoners, Dusty had sent Red to join their forward scout, under orders to reconnoitre and learn if the attack could be made without endangering Confederate property or lives. From what the red head had just said, he could continue with the bombardment.

"Make a map of how the land lies," Dusty ordered, for they were about a mile and a quarter from Little Rock and the rolling nature of the ground hid the town from his view. "No patrols out?"

"Nary a one," Red snorted and nodded to where the forward scout lay looking cautiously over a rim about three-quarters of a mile ahead. "Kiowa's riled, he allows the Yankees're selling him and us short not keeping watch."

With that he dismounted and, clearing a piece of ground, made a rough map of the area they hoped to bombard. Having completed his task, he collected his big brown horse which had been waiting patiently, ground-hitched by its dangling reins, mounted and rode back in the direction from which he had come.

Dusty studied the map for a moment, then looked towards his departing cousin. In his mind's eye, Dusty pictured the geography of the area. Then he turned and waved the two mortar wagons forward.

13

"Line them on Kiowa," he told the men leading the horses.

Although considering themselves the elite of the best damned *cavalry* regiment in the Confederate States' Army, the men detailed to act as gun crews sprang to their work with a will. The novel means of carrying the war to the enemy, combined with a desire to show the new Yankee general what kind of opposition faced him, gave zest to their movements. However, the two sergeants temporarily appointed chiefs-of-piece watched the men and controlled their high spirits.

Guiding the leading wagon, Sergeant Stormy Weather halted it so that its pole yoke lined directly at Kiowa Cotton on the distant rim. Sergeant Lou Bixby brought his wagon around until it stood alongside the other and also pointed in the required direction.

Normally the mortars would have been operated from a bed of stout timbers, to prevent the continued recoil sinking them into the ground and to facilitate altering the alignment or replacing them on the wagons when the time came to move on. Knowing that there would be time for at most three shots, and intending to destroy the platoon's equipment before he left, Dusty did not bother with such refinements. Going behind the wagons, he checked on their alignment. Each of the mortars weighed 1,852 pounds, so he wished to save his men from the exertion of using the handspikes to alter the aim as much as he could.

Satisfied, Dusty told the men to make ready the mortars. Weather and Bixby secured the ropes of the windlass at the rear of the wagons to the horns of the mortars, then unfastened the stout pins connecting the limber portions of the wagons to the rear sections which carried the weapons. While the limbers were being removed and the wagons' slip-ways lowered to the ground, Dusty joined Billy Jack's party by the caisson.

"Dang the luck!" the sergeant major moaned, watching two men lift an eighty-seven-and-a-half pound round shell —raising it between them in the grip of the specially-designed shell-tongs—from the forward of the three ammunition chests. "The blasted things're filled, so we can use them."

"Do you know how to?" Dust inquired.

"I figured you just stuck the shell in the hole 'n' hoped for the worst," Billy Jack answered languidly, taking a long, tapered wooden fuse from a box and studying the time-graduations marked down its length. "Likely they're all wrong and'll go off in the barrel."

"Don't you *ever* look on the bright side?" Dusty demanded.

"Sure I do. I 'member the last time real well. It was eight years, three months, two weeks 'n' four days back, come sundown. One of our good borrowing neighbours done fell down our well as he was coming calling."

"What happened?"

"It warn't the drinking well, so we figured it'd be a plumb waste of time to pull him out 'n' left him there," Billy Jack explained, then dropped his pose for a moment. "Range'd be around a mile 'n' a quarter, I reckon."

"Near enough," Dusty agreed. "Forty-five degrees elevation. We'll give 'em twenty seconds first go and alter it for the next if we're wrong."

"Should have a big enough target, anyways," the sergeant major drawled, using the point of his knife to pierce the wall of the fuse at the required graduation. "Or was you-all figuring on dropping the shells on top of Trumpeter's fool lil Yankee head?"

"I'll settle happy enough for scattering his review," Dusty answered.

With the fuses cut, he and Billy Jack fitted them carefully into the holes at the bottom of the shells. Ignited by the detonation of the main firing charge, the priming compound would burn down the inside of the wooden tube until reaching the opening cut by the sergeant major. There it would set off the five-pound bursting charge and explode the shell. While it did not work every time, the method gave a reasonable chance of success.

Wasting no time, the crews of the mortars had slid the pieces to the ground and removed the carriers. Selected for their strength, burly men wielded the handspikes and made adjustments to the directions in which the barrels pointed. Due to the care in positioning the wagons, they had little to do before Dusty announced his satisfaction. Removing the wooden tampions from the muzzles, the chiefs-of-piece gave the orders to load. First the powder charges went into the twenty-eight inch tubes and were rammed home. Then the men handling the tongs manoeuvred the shells into position.

Maybe the Texans did not move with the skilled precision of a trained artillery team, but they still carried out their duties at a good speed. Watching them, Dusty saw his earlier decision to have them trained to use artillery weapons justified. At the time it had been merely a means of keeping them occupied during a period when they were resting between patrols. The training was now paying off in that it allowed him to strike at the Yankees.

While the men completed the loading, Dusty looked about him. Two of his men stood some distance away, ready to cut the telegraph wires between Little Rock and Hot Springs and prevent warning of Company "C's" presence being sent ahead of them. Half-a-dozen more were headed west with the Yankee's platoon's horses, for the heavy draught animals would not be able to keep up with the Company's mounts in the event of a hurried departure. The remainder of the Company, less those employed on the mortars, kept watch on the surrounding country.

"Sure hope them fuses work like they should," Billy Jack said in a tone that hinted he doubted if they would. "Likely they'll make the shells burst in the barrel. Being so, I'll stand away somewheres safe. Like at the end of this-here lanyard."

Considering that the eight-foot log lanyard connected to the friction-primer in the right-side mortar's vent-hole, the gloomy prediction failed to worry the men who heard it. In fact Sergeant Stormy Weather hardly looked up from working the lever that tilted the barrel to the required angle of fire.

"All set, Cap'n Dusty!" announced the burly, jovial-featured Weather.

"Ready to go," confirmed the tall, dapper Sergeant Bixby by the other mortar.

"Let 'em go!" Dusty ordered.

Instantly Billy Jack and Bixby gave sharp tugs at their lanyard, operating the friction-primers. Steel rasped over the highly-combustible priming compound and ignited it, sending a spurt of flame into the powder grains of the main charge which turned rapidly into a terrific volume of gas. Set alight by the burning powder, the fuse began to operate. With a deep roar, the shell vomited from the left side mortar. A moment later, the second ball curved into the air.

Standing on the saluting base, General Trumpeter scowled as he watched the mass of men before him preparing to start the review. He frowned, thinking of the doubt he had seen on the faces of the senior officers under his command when he had spoken to them on the subject of his plans to defeat the Rebels. Maybe the Union Army's superior numbers, weapons and technology was swinging the War more and more in their favour on the other battle-fronts, but that did not apply in Arkansas. There the C.S.A. held firm and showed no sign of weakening. In fact, if the South had been able to send more men and equipment to Ole Devil Hardin, Trumpeter's colonels figured they would be hard-pressed to hold on to the land they had already taken.

In accordance with the policy of the Union's high command, the pick of the troops and weapons were reserved for the Eastern battle-zones. Most of the top brass favoured concentrating on striking down the heart of the Confederacy. After that had been accomplished, Texas—possibly the least affected of the Southern States by the major issues of the War—would be more ready to accept offers to surrender. So Arkansas had become garrisoned by green regiments, or those found wanting in the hard tests of combat. Poorly trained, demoralized by continual defeat, the men before Trumpeter were far from being ideal material for his dreams of conquest and fame. In fact he found himself doubting the wisdom of having so publicly stated his intentions when being assigned to take over the deceased General Buller's command.

Tall, slim, dark-haired, his handsome features were marred by a perpetual expression of arrogant superiority and an air of condescension. He made a fine figure in his smart blue dress uniform. Yet his military service did not extend beyond the start of the War and his background was not West Point but an Eastern civilian college. More politician than soldier, he had attained his rank with the patronage of powerful friends in the anti-slavery lobbies of his State's Legislature and the Federal Congress, aided by a chronic shortage of officers in the Union Army. For many years before the War, the Southern States had supplied the majority of the U.S. Army's officers, most of whom had returned to their homes on Secession. Few of the non-coms showed the necessary qualities to make officers, so the vacancies had been filled by men who at other times would have scorned to join the Army.

One of that kind, Trumpeter had passed rapidly up the promotion ladder, without any great effort or risk. Aware of the possibilities offered by a military acclaim when back in civilian life, Trumpeter had sought for a way by which he might reach the public's notice. Buller's death had offered it. There had been some reluctance among the other generals at taking over the unsuccessful Army of Arkansas. So Trumpeter's appointment met with no objections.

On his arrival, he had soon found that he faced a far more difficult task than he had imagined while riding a desk in far-off Washington. However, he possessed ideas that the routine-dulled brains of the career-soldiers could never have produced; two of which were already being put into effect. When they brought results, he would convince the weak-spined jellyfish before him that the Rebels across the Ouachita were no different from the other scum who formed the Confederate States. After which there would be replacements. Trumpeter meant to bring in men whose agreement with his "liberal" beliefs made them worthy of carrying out his schemes of conquest.

Trumpeter's scowl deepened as he studied the contingent from the 6th New Jersey Dragoons. On first meeting their colonel, he had mentioned his scheme to obtain remounts of a standard equal to that of the Rebel cavalry. Colonel Verncombe had expressed doubts that they could be delivered without strong escorts and would be subject to constant harassment or loss to the raiding Texans. So Trumpeter had not mentioned the plan he had thought out and already set into motion. He had hoped that the results of his brilliant scheme would make their appearance in time for the review, but they had not arrived. When they came, he could confound the doom-predicting Verncombe and—

An eerie double screech rose, growing louder by the second to chop through Trumpeter's thoughts. It was a sound which some of the men present recognized, although their general failed to identify it. Down from the sky curved a black ball and another followed it. Before Trumpeter had time to decide what was happening, the first shell exploded.

By accident, rather than deliberate, planned knowledge, the detonation of the first bursting charge took place at almost the ideal moment for maximum effectiveness. Exploding in the air about fifty yards above the centre of the assembled men, the shell sprayed a hail of .58 calibre musket balls on to them. Screaming and plunging, a horse went down while three men also fell. An instant after the first shell went off, the second burst and added its deadly cargo to that of its predecessor.

Coming so unexpectedly, the two shells threw the whole of the review into complete confusion. While the actual damage inflicted by the flying musket balls was not great, the side-effects proved to be all that Dusty could have desired. The cavalry and artillery suffered most. Caught in the process of mounting, men were flung from their startled, rearing horses. In the case of the cavalry, that meant only animals bolting with empty saddles; but the field artillery saw several of their cannon and caissons being dragged away by uncontrolled, frightened teams.

"Sponge those barrels out real careful!" Dusty warned his men, his eyes on Red who had rejoined Kiowa on the distant rim.

Plunging the sponge on the end of a ramrod pole into a wooden bucket filled with water, a good-looking private called Tracey Prince heard the words and grinned. He removed the sponge, shook it to get rid of excess water and thrust it into the barrel of the right side mortar to douse any remnants of burning powder. Not until he had checked that all was well did Sergeant Weather give the order to reload. Working just as fast and carefully, Sergeant Bixby's men recharged the second piece.

Seeing Red's obvious delight at the result of the first shots, Dusty made no alteration to the cutting of the second pair of fuses. Nor did he consider that the recoil had thrown the solid weight of the mortars sufficiently out of line to make any major corrections necessary.

Again the mortars boomed as he gave the order to fire. Standing behind them, Dusty saw that one shell was veering away from the other. It would not be far enough out of line to fall into the town, but he decided against chancing a further volley. He had no wish to continue the bombardment, with its indiscriminate slaughter. Having achieved his purpose of bearding General Trumpeter in the other's Little Rock den, Dusty intended to make good his escape. To have ruined the review and retired without loss or casualties would have a greater effect than staying until driven away by the Yankees.

"Stack the rest of the charges and shells around the mortars!" Dusty barked. "Bring the wagons and caissons up between the stove-pipes. I want everything wrecked when we leave."

In addition to meeting the agent, Dusty had been told to raid and do whatever damage he could while in enemy territory, so he had the means to destroy the loot completely. Red and Kiowa still remained on the rim, which meant that the Yankees had not yet organized a force to attack and drive Company "C" away. While his men carried out their orders, Dusty wondered what was happening outside the town.

All was confusion and pandemonium after the arrival of the first pair of shells. Fifty-five seconds later, before any semblance of order could be restored, the third shell burst in the air above the tangled, cursing mass of men. Having heard the banshee wailing of the shells' approach, discipline was forgotten and soldiers of all ranks flung themselves to the ground. Some of the cavalrymen who had managed to retain a hold of their horses' reins let loose and dived for safety. Trying to maintain control over his platoon, a lieutenant of Stedloe's Zouaves felt the wind of a close-passing musket-ball against his cheek. Fortunately for the future peace and security of the Sovereign State of Texas, 1st Lieutenant Jackson Marsden escaped without injury.*

Staring with fascinated horror, Trumpeter saw the second shell falling in his direction. Throwing himself from the saluting dais, he heard the missile explode and musket balls strike the stand he had quit an instant before. Rage filled him as he wondered which Rebel was responsible for the murderous attempt on his life. However, he stayed on the ground until sure that no other shells were coming.

Excited and amused by the chaos he saw displayed before him, Red Blaze did not forget his duty. There had been no attempt at organized reprisals and, studying the way the Yankees acted, none would be speedily forthcoming. So he nodded to the tall, lean sergeant at his side.

"I'd best go tell Cousin Dusty what's happened, Kiowa."

"Yo!" replied the other. "I'll stay on here a spell like Cap'n Dusty said."

Nobody, except possibly his mother, would have called Kiowa Cotton handsome. At best he looked like a particularly evil brave-heart Indian warrior hunting for the white-eye brother's scalp. Yet he as a good soldier, well-suited by birth and upbringing for the important duty of guiding Company "C" on their missions behind the enemy lines.

* The reason why is told in *The Devil Gun*.

Bare-headed, armed with a Remington Army revolver and bowie knife, he was to stay behind until pursuit was formed and sent after them, then take word of it to Dusty.

Collecting his horse, Red rode back to where Dusty was fitting the end of a coil of quick-match fuse into the hole in a shell. The men had worked fast and everything was as Dusty required by the time his cousin arrived.

"How'd it go, Cousin Red?" asked Dusty.

"You sure ruined his review," Red replied. "I haven't seen so much fussing, coming and going and running around since that time you and me brought a skunk to Cousin Betty's birthday party."

"Let's hope the Yankees don't catch us and lick us the way she did," Dusty grinned. Tommy Okasi had taught their cousin, Betty Hardin, to be proficient at *ju-jitsu* and *karate*.* On the occasion Red had mentioned, she put her lessons to good use in dealing out summary punishment to the offenders.

"They'll not be fixing to come after us for a spell yet," Red guessed. "You scattered the Dragoons and they're the best outfit Trumpeter's got. Need any help here, do you reckon?"

"Nope," Dusty decided, wedging the cord-like fuse into place. "Head out with the company. I'll catch up with you."

Riding off, Company "C" heard the roar of an explosion and, looking back, saw their leader approaching. Where the Yankee mortar platoon had been, only a large, smoking crater and scattered remnants of wood and metal remained. There was nothing of its equipment the Yankees could salvage.

---

* Betty's skill is demonstrated in *McGraw's Inheritance*.

CHAPTER THREE

Do I Ever Take Fool Chances?

"I bet ole Trumpeter's pot-boiling wild over us getting away from him after busting his review," Red Blaze enthused as he rode with Dusty Fog and Billy Jack ahead of the Company.

"He'll be after our hides for certain sure," Billy Jack agreed dolefully. "We should've told that Yankee luff we was Company "A"."

And have Trumpeter get all riled at Brother Buck? For shame," Red protested. "Let him 'n' Brother Pete find their own Yankee generals to get riled at 'em."

After firing the salute in General Trumpeter's honour, Dusty and his men had headed west at a good pace. By night-fall they had crossed the Saline River, making for the narrows which separated Lake Hamilton from Lake Ouachita. Kiowa had caught up shortly after they pulled out at dawn. He brought news that the Yankees had sent out a patrol three-companies strong, but it travelled slowly and would be unlikely to catch up with them. Nor would the garrison at Hot Springs be alerted to their presence. Not only had the telegraph wires been cut, but three long sections were carried out by the Texans. Trumpeter had sent a mounted courier with a message for the garrison commander at Hot Springs. However, Kiowa stated that he would not arrive. The spare horse, bearing a New Hampstead Volunteers' saddle, led by the scout gave confirmation to his statement.

Continuing their journey, and travelling at a speed possible only to master horsemen and first-class mounts, they crossed Garland County, avoiding the hamlets of Jessieville

23

and Mountain Valley. At no time did they see any sign of pursuit, nor had word of their coming reached Hot Springs, for no force came from the town to intercept them.

By mid-afternoon they were riding through the lightly wooded country parallel with but a mile from the northern shore of Lake Hamilton. The conversation between Red and Billy Jack ended abruptly as they saw the bare-headed Indian-dark Kiowa Cotton approaching from where he had been riding forward scout.

At a signal from Dusty, the fifty-strong main body of the company came to a halt. They needed no further orders, adopting a formation permitting an all-round defence should one prove necessary. The out-riding pickets to the rear and flanks also stopped, maintaining their vigil while awaiting instructions.

"Come across a bunch of fellers with some hosses up there by the narrows, Cap'n Dusty," Kiowa announced, halting his horse and getting as close to a salute as he offered to anybody.

"Soldiers?" Dusty asked.

"Ain't wearing uniforms if they are. Got maybe a hundred head of real good hosses and two wagons along. There's ten of 'em, toting what look like Burnside carbines and revolvers."

Digesting the information, Dusty nodded approvingly. Trust Kiowa to bring in all the pertinent details, such as the nature of the other party's armament. Burnside carbines, being single-shot, were not as dangerous as Spencer or Henry repeaters, but, firing metal-case cartridges, could be re-charged faster than a muzzle-loader. Such details were important in the event of a fight. Before Dusty could speak, Billy Jack injected the kind of comment they had come to expect from him.

"Could be a trap, Cap'n Dusty; 'n' when we spring it, they'll jump us and wipe us out to a man."

"What do you reckon, Cousin Red?' Dusty inquired, ignoring the gloomy words.

"If they're civilians, we'll have to go real careful," Red answered. "You mind what Uncle Devil told us about steering clear of doing anything the Yankee newspapers can call atrocities."

Since the start of the War, the Rebels and the Yankees had learned the uses of propaganda. Each side eagerly published stories of the other's atrocities, or blew up minor unsavoury incidents out of all proportion, as a means of stirring their people's patriotic indignation or creating an unfavourable image of the enemy to the rest of the world. Fully aware of how effective such propaganda could be, Ole Devil Hardin had given strict orders to his officers regarding their treatment of Union or non-aligned civilians they came across while on patrol.

"We'll go take a look, anyways," Dusty decided. "How does the land lie where they're camped, Kiowa?"

"They're out in the open, clear of the woods. We can get up to maybe a hundred yards of them without being seen. One thing I know for sure. There're no blue-bellies about. I looked real careful and if there is, they're hidden under the water 'n' not breathing enough to make bubbles."

Which meant that no Union force was watching the party by the narrows, ready to swoop on and destroy any Confederate patrol that made its appearance. However Dusty intended to take precautions.

"I'll come with you, Kiowa. Bring the company along after us, Cousin Red. Don't show yourselves until you figure I need you. And be ready for anything. I'd hate like hell to see Billy Jack get wiped out to a man."

"It'll come sooner or later, anyways," the gangling sergeant major replied. "So don't you go putting yourself out special on my account, Cap'n Dusty."

"What're them fellers doing, Kiowa?" Red asked.

"Making camp for the night, looked like," the scout answered. "They don't have any guards out, not even fellers riding herd on the hosses."

"They could be guerillas, Cousin Dusty," Red warned. "Don't you go taking any fool chances with them."

"Do I ever take fool chances?" Dusty smiled.

"Not more'n once a week," Red admitted.

"Trouble being," Billy Jack put in mournfully, "you ain't had your go at it yet this week."

Chuckling and promising to take care, Dusty rode off at Kiowa's side. Red gave the signal which spread the company into a mounted skirmishing line, then led them at a slower pace after his cousin. The main body had covered almost a mile when they saw their commanding officer and scout halt and dismount. Realizing that Dusty meant to study the mysterious party before going closer, Red further reduced the company's speed.

Leaving the horses ground-hitched, Dusty and Kiowa stalked cautiously to the edge of the woodland. Standing behind a stout old oak tree, they looked at the open ground bordering the narrows between the two lakes.

First Dusty examined the pair of wagons, standing with their teams unhitched. They appeared to be ordinary farm vehicles, with plain canopies that were open at the ends. From his position he could see into them. While they carried loads of some kind, they held neither concealed men nor weapons. That reduced the risk of the party acting as bait for a trap, a possibility Dusty had considered.

The horses took Dusty's attention next. As Kiowa had claimed, they were a fine selection. Gazing quietly on the rich grama grass behind the wagons and men, they stayed together in a way that hinted they had been long in each other's company. An exceptionally fine bay stallion was tethered clear of the others. Clearly the men trusted the horses to remain bunched, for nobody was riding herd on them.

So Dusty turned his eyes to the party gathered at the fire and saw what might be the answer to the lack of care. All but one were poorly dressed and looked like a gathering of town-dwelling manual workers who normally had small contact with horses. That they wore revolvers suspended at their sides—although not in such efficient holsters as the Texans sported—and had Burnside carbines stacked in neat pyramidal piles close by came as no surprise. Most men carried arms when travelling. Deserters, hunted by the military, often had to steal to stay alive. Worse than them, there were gangs of guerillas, who looted and pillaged under the guise of fighting for the Union or Confederacy, to make travelling hazardous. In fact, apart from the exception, the men might fall into one of these categories; although deserters or guerillas normally took greater precautions when in camp.

From all appearances, the exception was the party's leader. He wore a suit of big-city style, derby hat, spats and glossy shoes, but had removed his cravat and collar. The gunbelt about his waist looked out of place when taken with his warm, confiding, sunny cast of features. Short, round as a butterball, he exhibited an air of jovial respectability rarely, if ever, seen among the human wolves who called themselves "guerillas."

"Could be Yankee Soldiers," Kiowa remarked after a moment. "Their cavalry use plenty of Burnsides."

"Sure," Dusty agreed. "But civilians up north can likely buy them."

While most of the companies manufacturing firearms sought for bulk orders from the military, they augmented their profits by offering their products on the open market. The Burnside was a reasonably good gun, easy to operate and maintain and priced at a level within the reach of civilians. Finding so many of them together might be no more than coincidence. Even the fact that their owners had piled them military-fashion proved nothing, for the men could have seen soldiers doing it.

"What do you reckon then?" Kiowa wanted to know.

"I don't reckon they're blue-bellies disguised to trap us, but we'll play it careful," Dusty answered. "You and I'll go to them and hold their attention until the Company gets here."

Returning to their horses, they mounted. Dusty signalled for Red to keep coming. Then he and Kiowa passed out of the shelter of the trees. A big, burly man standing with the chubby dude saw them appear. Dropping his hand towards the flap of his holster, he growled a warning. Although most of the others showed anxiety, or reached for their revolvers, the dude displayed no alarm. Instead he spoke in a calm, reassuring manner and tapped the left side of his jacket. The words did not carry to Dusty's ears, but he saw the men refrain from drawing their weapons. Although they stood with empty hands, they formed a group behind the big man and scanned the woods beyond the approaching Texans with suspicious eyes.

Only the dude appeared completely unmoved by the arrival of the two Rebels. Leaving his companions, he padded almost daintily in the pair's direction as they halted their horses. While he seemed a mite puzzled—only to be expected when meeting Confederate soldiers so far in Union-held territory—he showed neither animosity nor concern.

"Good afternoon, gentlemen," the dude greeted in a cultured New England accent, darting a glance beyond them. "Welcome to our camp. If you wish to have a meal, feel free to join us." He paused then continued, "Are you alone?"

"My Company's about a mile back," Dusty answered, confident that Red would keep the men hidden and not give the lie to the words. He swung to the ground and went on, "Mind if I ask who you are and what you're doing here?"

"Understandable questions both, sir. My name is Oswald Lomax Hoffinger and I am leading this party of recently-arrived immigrants to join their families in New Mexico."

"Can you prove it?" Dusty inquired, knowing that Kiowa was watching the men.

"Of course, sir," Hoffinger agreed. "I have a document in my pocket, if I may be permitted to produce it—"

"Go to it," Dusty offered.

For all his pompous manner, the dude had the good sense to give a warning before letting his hand go out of sight under his jacket. Reaching across to his inside breast pocket, Hoffinger brought out a sheet of paper. While opening it and holding it to Dusty, he spoke in a foreign language, addressing the words to his companions as they stood scowling at the Texans.

"I was merely informing them that all is well, Captain," Hoffinger declared, smiling disarmingly. "None of the poor fellows speak English and all are concerned by your arrival."

"Maybe they've cause to be," Dusty said.

"They have not, sir," Hoffinger stated before Dusty could do more than glance at the paper. "In fact you might almost say that I'm helping the Confederate States. I'm taking these able-bodied men away from the fighting. They had been tricked into enlisting in the Union Army, poor fellows, but my organization—you've probably heard of us, the Society For The Preservation of Human Rights—?"

"I can't say I have," Dusty grunted and started reading.

Bearing the official printed heading of the Department of the Interior, the document stated the O. L. Hoffinger, secretary of the Society For the Preservation Of Human Rights, had permission to escort the "under-named" men to the Territory of New Mexico and that they and their property must not be taken into service by any officer of the United States' Army. Everything about the paper seemed authentic enough, although Dusty could not vouch for the validity of the signature on it.

"I trust that this explains our position to your satisfaction, Captain." Hoffinger said when he saw that Dusty had finished reading.

"Not all the way," Dusty replied.

"Then permit me to clarify it somewhat. Word reached my Society of the scandalous way in which these poor fellows had been treated. Naturally we set about obtaining their freedom as they had been enlisted by fraud. We are not without influence in Congress, and succeeded. Their families had already gone to take up their homes, so it was decided that I should accompany them and ensure that they reached their destination without further interference."

"How about the horses?"

"Bought before their enlistment, as the means of tilling their farms. We insisted that the Army returned them and once again justice prevailed. How could they plough their land without horses?"

"Mind if I talk to them?" Dusty asked, ignoring the question.

"Feel free—Do you speak German?"

"Nope," Dusty admitted, studying the men. None of them had Teutonic or Anglo-Saxon features and coloration. "Are they Germans?"

"From various parts of mid-Europe. Polish mostly. But Mr. Glock there speaks German well enough for me to communicate with them through him."

Walking towards the fire, accompanied by Hoffinger, with Kiowa prowling alert for danger on their heels, Dusty thought over what he had been told. All the men were of military age and in good health. With an urgent need for extra troops, it seemed unlikely that the Union Army would release potential recruits. Yet they might if sufficient political pressure was brought to bear. The North was infested by "liberal" organizations for the protection of the "down-trodden," some of which was one of the more influential, the Army might yield to its wishes as a gesture of good will. Especially with the men unable to speak English, rendering training them difficult. In one way the number of Burnside carbines strengthened the story. Possibly the Society had obtained a reduction in price by buying in bulk. Having obtained the men's release, the Society would waste no time in reuniting them with their families and might even send one of their senior officials, armed with suitable authority, to act as an escort.

From an officer in the C.S.A.'s viewpoint, Dusty considered that the men would be of less use to the Union as farmers in New Mexico than by serving in the Yankee Army. He could also imagine how the North's newspapers would blow up the story if Hoffinger had told the truth and he took the horses from their owners.

Yet all the horses, particularly the big bay stallion, looked far more suitable for riding than performing the dragging and hauling of farm work.

Then a thought struck Dusty as he approached the big man called Glock. It was a small matter, maybe, but significant in view of Hoffinger's story. New Mexico lay to the west, yet the trace-poles at the front of the wagons were pointing eastwards. While the springy grama grass did not lend itself to retaining tracks that proved otherwise, Dusty doubted if Hoffinger's party would turn their wagons to face the direction from which they had come when making camp for the night.

So far none of the men Dusty approached had been shown that they knew his Company was close at hand, but he felt sure that Red was already in position. Which meant he must make his move before Glock's bunch discovered their presence.

Suddenly, giving no hint of his intentions, Dusty stepped close and stamped as hard as he could on Glock's right foot. Letting out a startled howl, the big man hopped on his left leg, clutched at his throbbing toes and acted just as the small Texan hoped that he might.

"What the hell do you reckon you're—!" Glock roared in a language Dusty and Kiowa could understand, chopping off his words as he realized what he was doing.

"Man," drawled the Indian-dark scout, tensing ready to back his captain's play. "You sure learned to talk English fast."

Aware of what he had done, Glock slammed his aching foot to the ground. At the same time, he stabbed his right hand towards the flap of his holster. Behind him, the other men just stood and stared. Even Hoffinger appeared to be shocked into immobility by Dusty's actions.

Dusty knew that Glock would be unable to draw the revolver at any speed, so he decided against gun-play as a means of halting the attempt. While Dusty could easily have fetched out one or both his Colts and shot Glock, he knew doing so might spark off a full-scale fight.

Not that he feared for his own safety. At the first hint of trouble, Red had brought the Company out of the trees. They were now galloping forward, guns in hand, so that the men behind Glock would be wiped out before any could offer more than a token resistance. Taking no pleasure in killing, Dusty did not want that to happen. Especially when there was a more satisfactory way of handling the situation. Without ever having heard of psychology, he guessed that capturing some of the enemy, then releasing them disarmed but uninjured, would carry a greater morale impact than leaving them dead. By treating them so leniently he would emphasize to the captives, and their comrades-in-arms, the superiority of the Confederate States Army in Arkansas.

So Dusty left his guns in the holsters and relied, as he had against Savos, on Tommy Okasi's training. He did not use the *tegatana*, handsword, but brought off one of the even more effective *keriwaza* kicking attacks. Measuring the distance between himself and Glock, he balanced on his right leg and launched his left foot into the air. Curling his toes upwards as far as possible, he flexed his ankle and propelled the ball of his foot with considerable force against the pit of the big man's stomach.

Glock slammed backwards and doubled over. Jerking the hand from the unopened holster, he clutched at his mid-section. Winded and filled with nausea, he was in no condition to defend himself against the continuation of the attack. Following the man up, Dusty drove his clenched right first in a power-packed backhand swing to the centre of the other's face. Lifted erect by the impact, Glock pitched helplessly into the arms of the men behind him.

From delivering the blow, Dusty whipped his right arm down and over so his fingers grasped the butt of the left side Colt. Already his left hand was curling about the bone handle of the other revolver. Steel rasped on leather, merging with the clicks of the hammers being drawn back to full cock. In three-quarters of a second from Dusty starting his draw, the men into whom Glock had collided were looking down the barrels of his Army Colts. The manner in which he had handled Glock left them almost numb with amazement and he did not intend to grant them time to recover.

"Don't move, any of you!" Dusty warned.

And, in some strange way, he no longer looked small. Instead he gave the impression of possessing size and bulk sufficient to tower above them all. Such was the force of his personality that, taken with his fast-drawn Colts, he prevented the men from attempting to resist.

Knowing Dusty, Kiowa had expected him to do something and had been ready to take a hand when he did. Even as Dusty stamped on Glock's toe, Kiowa had slid out his bowie knife. When Hoffinger made as if to move forward, Kiowa caught him by the scruff of the neck from behind. Bringing the dude to a halt, Kiowa pricked his plump ribs with the clip point of the knife and breathed a savage warning.

"You-all too fat to tangle with Cap'n Dusty."

"That, I assure you, was never my intention," Hoffinger croaked, staring in fascinated awe at the result of Dusty's attack.

Releasing the dude's neck, but keeping the knife in position, Kiowa reached around to pluck the Le Mat revolver from Hoffinger's holster. The rest of the Company came up, most of them bringing their horses to sliding halts and lining their weapons at the dude's men. Sergeant Weather led half-a-dozen soldiers towards the unattended horses, ready to control them should there be shooting. The precaution was unnecessary. So effectively did the Texans surround the other party that resistance would have been suicidal.

"Disarm them, Mr. Blaze!" Dusty ordered. "Billy Jack, take four men and search those wagons."

"I think that I had better tell you the truth, Captain," Hoffinger called, being prevented by Kiowa from going closer to the small Texan.

"I was just figuring to ask you to do that," Dusty replied, watching his orders carried out. "Let him come, Kiowa."

Scuttling gratefully away from the Indian-dark sergeant, who he felt wanted only an excuse to take his scalp, Hoffinger came to Dusty's side and dropped his voice in a confiding manner.

"The fact of the matter is, Captain, that we have stolen those horses and deserted from the Union Army and are headed west of New Mexico to start a new life."

CHAPTER FOUR

Line Five Up and Shoot Them

"Deserters, huh?" Dusty grunted, twirling away his Colts.

"From the Union Army, sir," Hoffinger confirmed. "This is a carefully planned desertion, hence the spurious document which you thrust into your tunic before testing my men."

"Why'd you lie about it when we rode up then?"

"Merely to ascertain how the document and story would stand up under the scrutiny of an alert, efficient officer like yourself. I had, of course, every intention of telling you the truth after you had tested my companions' ability to act as newly-arrived immigrants who speak no English. You produced a remarkably effective way of testing them, I must say."

Every word Hoffinger spoke had a ring of truth to it, while his whole being exuded an aura of sincerity. So much so that Dusty felt suspicious. Yet he admitted that his feelings might stem from antipathy to smooth-talking, portly dudes, or even out of his dislike for deserters.

"That's how it is, huh?" Dusty said.

"Exactly how it is, sir," Hoffinger confirmed. "And an officer of your undoubted experience can visualize the effect on the Union Army in Arkansas when words gets out that there has been such a large desertion. More so when the soldiers learn that, in accordance with General Hardin's policy, the deserter were given free passage for themselves and their horses by members of the Texas Light Cavalry."

"I see. We're going to let you fellers go and take those horses with you."

"In return for which I will gladly append my signature to a statement that you have done so. When news of it—"

"Drop it, *hombre!*" Dusty snapped, his entire attitude changing to one of cold annoyance. "You're not deserters."

"But I assure you we are, sir!" protested Hoffinger. "We are tired of fighting for a cause in which we no longer believe. So we are going to New Mexico—"

"Then how come your wagons are pointed east?" Dusty countered and looked at Hoffinger's men. "Are you bunch deserters?"

Sullen faces glared at him and Glock, removing a hand from his bloody nose, answered in a surly tone.

"Yeah. And Ole Devil Hardin allowed any Yankee who deserted could take his guns and hosses with him without having 'em took off him by Rebel soldiers."

A point which Dusty had been considering ever since Hoffinger had mentioned that they were deserters. Both sides had used such inducements as safe passage through their lines, or offers of homes and employment, to encourage desertion by the other's soldiers and sailors. So Ole Devil had given orders that his men would in no way interfere with deserters from the Union Army.

If Hoffinger had told the truth, Dusty could not confiscate the horses. Capture of the dude's party by the Yankees would be almost inevitable if he did. Dusty could imagine the delight displayed by various Northern newspapers at receiving proof that the Rebels did not keep their promises to deserters. The story would have an adverse effect in Arkansas, where desertion caused a steady drain on the Federal man-power. Even worse to Dusty's way of thinking, it would imply that his uncle—for whom he felt the greatest admiration and respect—could not be relied upon to keep his word.

Once again Dusty knew that he must step warily. Maybe the Yankees, plagued by desertion, had sent out Hoffinger's party to prove that the Rebels in the field did not honour their commanding general's offers of co-operation to deserters. Unlikely, perhaps, but Dusty wanted to be certain before taking any action.

"I reckon that you're guerillas, not deserters!" Dusty stated and looked where Red stood listening. "What do you say, Mr. Blaze?"

"They're stinking border-jumpers for sure, sir," Red answered, judging that an affirmative reply was expected and obliging. "I can smell it on them."

"We're deserters!" Hoffinger insisted, seeing his men show signs of concern.

"The hell you are!" Dusty barked. "They're guerillas, Mr. Blaze."

"Yes, sir! And Un—General Hardin gave orders that we shot any of 'em we caught. Say now! I heard tell that some of Quantrill's boys had got to arguing which killed best, an Enfield or a Sharps. To settle it, they lined up five prisoners to see how many of 'em each gun'd shoot through."

"I heard about that," Dusty said thoughtfully, showing none of the delight he felt at the way Red had caught on to and improved upon his scheme.

"I was wondering which'd shoot best out of my Henry 'n' these Burnsides," Red remarked in a speculative manner. "Seeing's how we're going to kill this bunch, I just might's well find out."

"Hey now—!" Glock began, but was held back by the Texan guards.

"Go to it," Dusty said. "Line five up and shoot them, Mr. Blaze."

Shock creased the prisoners' faces as Red swung eagerly towards them. The inhuman experiment carried out by members of William Clarke Quantrill's guerilla band had been given much publicity in the North. Clearly all Hoffinger's men had heard and believed the story. Nor did they doubt, looking at him, that Red was not only willing but eager to duplicate the trial on their bodies. Only the dude remained calm. Standing at Dusty's side, he smiled and opened his mouth. Before Hoffinger could speak, Glock came to a military brace and saluted the small Texan.

"We're soldiers, Cap'n,'" the big man declared. "I'm

Sergeant-major Glock of the New Hampstead Volunteers and these fellers're from my company."

"How about that, Mr. Hoffinger?" Dusty asked.

"We are deserters—" the dude insisted.

"Prove it," Red challenged, "and fast. I'm wanting to try these guns."

"I can hardly produce a document from the Army to say we've deserted," Hoffinger protested.

"Damn it, we're the official escort for these remounts, Cap'n!" Glock yelled, indicating the horses. "Being dressed this way's part of a fool notion Hoffinger thought out."

"Can you *prove* that?" Dusty drawled, while Red fingered a Burnside longingly.

"Of course we ca—!" Hoffinger began.

"Show him that paper, you crazy son-of-a-bitch!" Glock roared being restrained from springing forward by the lined guns of the guards. "They ain't fooling."

"Damn it!" Red growled. "I'm tired of this talking. Cut out five of 'em, Sergeant Bixby, and send a man for my Henry."

"No!" Glock bellowed and his men added their voices to the plea. "Cap'n, he's got another letter, telling the truth about us. It's in the 'grape-shot'—"

"You stupid bastard!" wailed Hoffinger. "Why didn't you call their bluff? Neither of them aimed to go through with it."

"Didn't we?" Dusty asked. "Let me have Mr. Hoffinger's revolver, Kiowa."

"I doubt very much if you did, sir," the dude answered, knowing that Dusty had read correctly the meaning of Glock's last sentence, interrupted though it had been. "By the 'C' on your guidon, I assume that you are Dusty Fog. Unfortunately I failed to see it in time to announce the fact."

"Hell's teeth, yes!" Glock spat out. "If I'd known—"

Ignoring the comments, Dusty examined the revolver. Due to a lack of manufacturing facilities in the South, Colonel Alexandre Le Mat had gone to France to produce his revolvers. Sufficient of them had been smuggled through the U.S. Navy's blockade on the Confederate ports for Dusty to be familiar with their peculiarities. The gun he held was a standard production model. Under the .40 calibre hexagonal barrel was a second shorter and larger tube. At its rear end, this tube acted as a base-pin for the nine-shot cylinder and was, in fact, a smooth-bore barrel designed to fire a .50 calibre "grape-shot" ball.

However Hoffinger's Le Mat did not carry its lethal secondary load. Inserting the tip of his little finger, Dust eased a rolled sheet of paper out of the "grape-shot" barrel. It proved to be an authorization for Hoffinger to collect one hundred remounts and deliver them to the U.S. Army of Arkansas' headquarters. In the next paragraph, Sergeant-major Glock and the escort were permitted to travel in civilian clothes. Lastly, all Union Army officers were required to give the party every assistance by order of General Horace Trumpeter.

Watching Dusty read the document, Hoffinger wondered if there was any way in which the situation might yet be saved. Annoyance filled the chubby dude. Not so much at the failure to trick Dusty, although that rankled a little, but because he had made the mistake of under-estimating an opponent's potential. To a man in Hoffinger's profession, such a mistake was inexcusable.

Hoffinger had started life as a petty thief, graduating to the more genteel status of confidence trickster by virtue of his native talents. A man by nature peace-loving, he had avoided active participation in the War. Hovering safely clear of the fighting, he had managed to garner a comfortable living. Circumstances, not unconnected with a supply-contracts swindle in the process of going wrong, made a change of scenery of vital importance. The western "hinter-lands" had seemed the best choice when good fortune presented him with the chance of getting there and making money without too much work or risk.

It had all begun when he learned that General Trumpeter had obtained permission to purchase remounts from the Pawnee Indians. Officers with considerable experience of

conditions in Arkansas had warned that collecting the
horses would be fraught with difficulties. In fact, the general consensus of military opinion had been that purchases
from that source would be a waste of time and money, with
the results not worth the cost. The unanimity of their views
merely served to convince Trumpeter that he was right and
he looked for a way to prove it.

A keen student of human nature, Hoffinger felt that he
knew how to deal with Trumpeter. By sycophantic agreement and professing "liberal" learnings, the dude had convinced the general that he was the man most suitable to
collect the horses. Hoffinger had suggested using a small
escort, dressed in civilian clothes and backed by the fake
document as a means of tricking any Rebel patrol which
met them; although he had been glib enough to make it
appear the idea came from Trumpeter. Seeing a way to
prove the career-officers wrong, Trumpeter had needed little convincing. If a man like Hoffinger succeeded, the general figured that he would have a powerful weapon to wave
in the faces of his critics.

Patriotic fervour had not prompted Hoffinger's actions.
He had seen a way out of his difficulties and means to start
a profitable career. Up until the meeting with Dusty Fog,
everything had been satisfactory. As well as collecting the
horses, he had made useful contacts and picked up some
easily-sold merchandise. So he had hoped for further missions, with the Army paying his expenses and providing an
escort to ensure his safety. At least they had on the first
trip. He could not see there being others if he failed to
deliver the horses.

"This's about what I'd figured it'd be," Dusty drawled,
folding the paper and placing it with the another "authorization" in his tunic's inside pocket. "You'd show it to any
Yankee officer who wouldn't accept your 'Society' story,
I'd say."

"That is correct, sir," Hoffinger agreed. "I might have
needed proof that we aren't deserters or guerillas."

"Likely General Trumpeter reckoned if a civilian could

bring in his horses, it'd show his men that us Rebs aren't
so all-fired tough or smart after all."

"I couldn't say about that," Hoffinger answered tact-
fully.

"Did you figure anybody'd fall for that story you told
me?"

"I've always found the more unlikely the story, if it is
backed by documentary proof, the more likely it is to be
accepted. You might have accepted it yourself if I'd
thought to have the wagons turned to face west when we
halted."

"Could be," Dusty admitted. "Not having pickets out
helped your story, soldiers would have. I'd've thought
twice before taking horses from civilians when they'd got
what'd read in a Yankee newspaper like a real good reason
for needing 'em."

"What's in the wagons, Billy Jack?" Red asked, seeing
the sergeant-major ambling disconsolately towards them, a
large buck-skin trailing in his hand.

"Food, bed-rolls 'n' such in the first 'n'. I've had all
their ammunition put on the hosses. T'others toting buffalo
hides, Injun moccasins and such—"

"They're mine, Captain Fog!" Hoffinger interrupted.
"And so is that money—"

"This here, Cap'n Dusty," Billy Jack went on, holding
out the bag. "Found it hid in the second wagon."

"It's mine!" Hoffinger insisted. "All I have in the world.
I staked all my savings on this collecting mission and that's
all that remains."

"Give it to him, Billy Jack," Dusty said. "We don't rob
civilians. Let's go take a look at the horses."

"Why not share a meal with us first, Captain?" Hoffinger suggested. "We've enough food for you."

"Thanks for the offer," Dusty replied. "That's what
we'll do."

During the meal, Hoffinger studied Dusty and revised
his previous ideas. The earlier crude flattery had been
aimed at a naïve younger holding rank by family influence.
Now Hoffinger knew better. Young he might be, but the

small Texan controlled those hard-bitten veterans by virtue of his personality and achievements.

Looking around, Hoffinger noticed that the Texans continued performing their duties with the minimum of supervision. While he entertained the officers by the wagon carrying his property, Hoffinger saw Billy Jack and Kiowa seated talking amiably to Glock and Corporal Mullitz. Staring at the latter, Hoffinger felt the start of an idea. A long chance, maybe, but infinitely better than no chance at all. Quickly he turned back to his guests, not wanting them to become aware of his interest in Mullitz. During the rest of the meal, he put together the details of his scheme.

"Thanks for the food, Mr. Hoffinger," Dusty said at last, coming to his feet. "Have the men get ready to pull out while I look at the horses, Cousin Red."

"They're all good stock," Hoffinger put in. "Except for the bay stallion, that is. He won't be any use to you."

"Why not?" Red inquired with interest.

"He was sent by a Pawnee chief as a gift for General Trumpeter. But I fear that he is unmanageable."

"I've yet to see the horse that couldn't be managed," Red remarked.

"This one can't," Hoffinger stated before Dusty could speak. "In fact I'm willing to bet that you haven't a man here who can saddle and ride it, even though the chief assured me it had been saddle-broke and one of his men rode it in from the tribe's horse-herd."

"You'd bet on it?" Dusty asked quietly.

"I would, sir. And I have a thousand dollars in gold to back my words."

"A thousand dollars," Dusty said. "Against what?"

"The remounts," Hoffinger told him.

"That's a right sporting bet!" Red snorted. "The hosses're worth more than a thousand dollars."

"True," Hoffinger replied. "But I have seen the horse ridden and feel that I should be given odds."

"The hell—!" Red started hotly.

"He's right," Dusty interrupted. "If that chief told the truth, he should have the odds. So if Mr. Hoffinger fetches out that thousand dollars, I'll take his bet and give it a whirl."

Hoffinger held down the delight he felt at Dusty falling into the trap. He did not doubt that the bet would be honoured and, considering how the horse had acted when his men tried to saddle it, was sure that Dusty would fail.

"The money's in my hand, sir," Hoffinger said, holding out the bag. "Mr. Blaze will be acceptable to me as stakeholder."

"We'll let Sergeant-major Glock help him," Dusty answered. "Red, tell Sandy to fetch over my saddle while I take a look at the horse."

Leaving Red to attend to the details, Dusty went to where the bay was tethered. Swinging to face him, it backed off until halted by the rope. Ears pricked and nostrils flaring, it exhibited a nervousness which increased as Sandy McGraw came up carrying Dusty's saddle, saddle-blanket and bridle. A jingle from the latter's bit brought a louder snort and the horse reared as high as the picket rope would let it.

"Put the blanket and saddle down, Sandy," Dusty ordered in a quiet, gentle voice. "And take the bridle away with you."

The guidon-carrier obeyed and as he retired, Billy Jack passed him walking with greater than usual speed.

"Hear tell you've bet you can ride that hoss, Cap'n Dusty," the sergeant-major said. "Got to talking to Fritz Glock about it just now. He reckons the Pawnee Chief they got it off allowed it'd been three-saddled. Only neither him nor Joe Mullitz've managed to get a saddle on its back or bit in its mouth."

"Sounds bad," Dusty drawled, knowing that "three-saddled" meant the horse had been ridden at least three times by the man breaking it.

"Don't you sell'em short. They're both thirty-year men and trained as cavalry afore the War. Mullitz was a riding instructor back East."

"Did he ever serve out West?"

"Neither him nor Fritz from what they told us."

"That figures," Dusty said cryptically. "Let's see if I can win that bet."

"Ole Devil'll have your hide if you lose!" Billy Jack wailed and, for once, his concern was not entirely assumed, for he knew the stakes of the wager.

"Likely," Dusty admitted. "Tell Glock's men I figured the New Hampstead Volunteers're sporting enough not to make fuss and spoil my chance."

"Sure," Billy Jack answered. "And in case they ain't sporting enough, I'll have 'em watched real good."

Turning his attention to the horse once more, Dusty noticed that its nervousness had died slightly with the removal of the jingling bridle. As he expected, it had on an Indian hackamore and not a U.S. Army halter. The chief difference was that the former had reins attached to a *bosal*—a rawhide loop fitted around the face just above the mouth—instead of a lead-rope.

Although Sandy had removed Dusty's bed-roll and sabre on hearing of the bet, he had left the rope strapped to the saddle horn. Taking it, Dusty walked slowly towards the horse. Snorting and pawing the ground, it watched him suspiciously. All the time, he kept up a flow of soft-spoken, soothing talk. With the picket rope knotted to the *bosal,* he could not flip his loop over the bay's head. Instead he slid the stem of his Manila rope across the top of its neck. Catching the end of the stem underneath the neck, he quickly formed a running noose and drew it tight.

Naturally the news of the bet had attracted considerable attention. Recalling their non-coms' experiences with the bay, Glock's men waited to see how Dusty would fare. Equally interested, the Texans kept clear of their prisoners and remained alert for trouble. Neither Red nor Billy Jack looked too happy about the affair, being aware of what might happen to Dusty should he lose.

A smile played on Hoffinger's lips as he watched the rope tighten about the horse's neck. Then it wavered and died. Instead of fighting to tear free, the bay stood still. Keeping the rope taut, Dusty backed until he could pick up his saddle and blanket. Still moving unhurriedly, he returned with them in his hand. The horse let out another snort, yet did not fight against the rope. Up close, Dusty set down his saddle. Then he caressed the bay's head with his hands, stroking its nostrils and eyes before taking hold of the head-piece of the *bosal*. Keeping the head steady, he leaned forward and began to blow into its flaring nostrils.

"What's he do—!" Hoffinger yelped, the words ending as Red rammed an elbow into his ribs.

"You try yelling to spook the hoss again," Red growled in a low savage tone, "and I'll raise lumps all over your pumpkin head with my Colt's butt."

Knowing that his escort meant to carry out the threat, Hoffinger lapsed into silence. Yet, to give him his due, surprise rather than any foul motive had caused the outburst. He had been amazed by the bay's lack of resistance and at Dusty's actions.

After standing by the horse's head for a short time, Dusty took up his saddle. Anticipation bit at Hoffinger, mingled with the thought that something was wrong. Not until Dusty had slid the folded blanket into place did the dude realize what it was. With growing delight, he saw that the small Texan was standing on the right side of the horse instead of at the left. Yet the bay showed none of its usual objections to either the blanket or the saddle, despite the change of procedure. Not even the adjustment of the girths about its belly provoked the kind of savage protests which had met attempts by Glock or Mullitz to saddle it. Instead it stood quietly and allowed Dusty to unfasten the picket-rope from the *bosal*.

"He's not using a bridle or a bit!" Hoffinger croaked, watching Dusty slip his right foot into the stirrup iron and swing astride the bay.

"Danged if he's not forgot," grinned Red, knowing that the *bosal* served as a bit and beginning to realize why Dusty had accepted the bet.

Settling on the saddle, Dusty felt the horse tense itself between his legs. Gripping the reins in his right hand, he cautiously freed his rope. A nudge with his heels sent the bay off in a long "straight-away" buck. Although it sailed high, it came down without twisting, whirling or the dangerous powerful hindquarter's kick that could drive the base of the rider's spine against the cantle of the saddle. Performed without the refinements, bucking straightaway posed no problems for a man with Dusty's skill. In fact he soon realized that his mount was doing no more than try him out. It continued to crow-hop for a short time. The see-saw motion of the bucking looked spectacular, but required little effort to ride out. Nor did it sustain the fight and it soon began to respond to the messages of the reins.

"I—I don't believe it!" Hoffinger croaked as Dusty rode towards him.

At the same time, the dude knew that his last chance had gone. Even the hope that his escort would take advantage of their captors' preoccupation, jump and overcome them, did not materialize. All Glock's men sat under guard, staring with open-mouth amazement and apparently frozen into immobility by the ease with which the small Texan had mastered the hitherto unmanageable stallion.

"My bet, I reckon," Dusty drawled, halting the horse. Swinging his left leg forward and over the saddle horn, he dropped to the ground at the bay's right side. "Sandy, put my rig back on the black."

"And see you take it off the bay from the Indian-side," Red advised, grinning as he took the bag of money from Glock's limp hand.

"*Indian*-side?" Hoffinger repeated.

"Why sure," Dusty said. "Didn't you fellers notice that the Indians always saddle-up and mount from the right, instead of at the left like white folks?"

"I didn't," Hoffinger began. "From the ri—But that means—"

"Yeah," agreed Dusty. "Every time your men tried to saddle it from the left, they spooked it. Trying to use a bit made things worse. Indins don't use 'em."

"Way you look on," Red continued, "I reckon you figured Dusty'd rile it up by putting a rope 'round its neck."

"I did," Hoffinger admitted, surprised to learn that the youngster had read his emotions so well.

"An Indian breaks his horse by roping it and choking it down," Red explained. "That's rough on the horse and after he's felt it a couple of times he learns better'n fight against a running noose. After the horse gets over being choked down, the Injun fusses it a mite and blows into its nostrils. Damned if I know why, but doing that quietens it down and lets him know the feller doing it's his friend."

"You still took a risk," Captain Fog," Hoffinger pointed out. "Even counting on us not knowing which side to saddle and mount from, the Pawnee chief could have been lying about it being fully saddle-broken."

"Indians don't do a heap of lying," Dusty answered. "And I figured it was near on certain he hadn't, the bay being a chief's gift for General Trumpeter."

"I'm afraid that I still don't understand."

"Figure it this way. That chief's got plenty of horses to sell and's likely getting a better price from you than he could any other place—"

"The price is adequate, I admit, but I still don't follow your reasoning."

"It's easy enough," Dusty told him. "The chief wants to keep General Trumpeter friendly and eager to buy more horses. So he sends along a gift. Now he doesn't know how good a rider the general is, so he figures not to take chances. The horse he picks looks good, has some spirit, but's real easy and gentle to ride. That's the way I saw it and reckoned I could win the bet easy. The South can use a thousand dollars in Yankee gold, only I couldn't take it from a civilian by force, now could I?"

"Well, I'm damned!" Hoffinger croaked. "You've slickered me, Captain Fog!"

"They do say it's hell when it happens to you," Dusty replied with a grin. "I want to pull out in fifteen minutes, Cousin Red."

"Yo!" Red replied and walked away grinning.

Once again Cousin Dusty had pulled it off. Sure Red and Billy Jack knew how Indians trained and mounted their horses; but neither of them had thought out a way to put their knowledge to use. Dusty had done so and gained a large sum of money for which the Confederate States' Secret Service could probably find a purpose. What was more, he had done it in a way which the Yankee newspapers could not call robbing a civilian. Glock and the others were sure to talk of the bet on their return and would be believed no matter how the Union tried to prevent it.

In fifteen minutes, the Company was ready to march. Smiling, Hoffinger, held out his hand to the small Texan who had bested him.

"I hope General Trumpeter's not too riled at you for losing the remounts," Dusty said, shaking hands. "Tell him from me that we'll likely need them in our retreat across the Red River."

"That's one excuse I won't use," chuckled Hoffinger. "I feel that by now he will be very touchy when that particular stream is mentioned. Good-bye, Captain Fog. With no disrespect, sir, I hope our paths don't cross again."

"They might if you try to fetch in more of these remounts," Dusty warned.

"That is a remote contingency, sir," Hoffinger sighed. "My continued employment depended on delivering this bunch."

"I'm real sorry to spoil it for you," Dusty said. "But I reckon a feller as talented as you'll find some way of earning his living. *Adios.*"

"That young man is going to annoy General Trumpeter before he's through," Hoffinger told Glock as they watched the Texans drive the horses into the water.

"He's already done it," Glock answered, fingering his stomach and grinning with grudging admiration. "Damned if he didn't fire a salute for the general, Billy Jack told me. Out of two of *our* mortars and right into the middle of a review Trumpeter was holding. Yes sir, Mr. Hoffinger, Trumpeter's going to hate Dusty Fog's name."

CHAPTER FIVE

We've Got to Stop Those Guns!

"There's something up, Mr. Blaze!" growled grizzled old Corporal Vern Hassle, bringing his horse to a sliding halt after returning at speed to the four-man scouting party sent ahead to learn what force of Yankees guarded the Snake Ford of the Caddo.

It was almost noon on the day following the capture of Hoffinger's horses and Company "C" were travelling south-east as fast as they could manage accompanied by the remounts and heavy draught animals. They had seen no sign of pursuit, but Kiowa kept watch on their back-trail. The previous night, in camp, Dusty and Red had studied their maps and decided where they could best make their crossing into Rebel territory.

Every ford along the Caddo and Ouachita Rivers was guarded by detachments of Confederate and Union troops. In addition, both sides kept patrols moving along the rivers' banks to watch for infiltration by the enemy. On their way out, Company "C" had crossed at an unguarded stretch of fast-flowing water through which only expert horsemen could pass. Using the same place on their return would be dangerous for they had a large bunch of riderless horses with them. To make a crossing would be a lengthy process and leave them open to attack should a Yankee patrol locate them.

While there had been two fords closer, Dusty had selected Snake Ford. The other two had to be approached across open, level ground with no chance of taking the Yankees by surprise. Snake Ford lay in a wide, winding valley. Being of little military importance, it was held by a

49

company of Stedloe's Zouaves and a platoon of Dragoons. On the other side, a full battalion of Arkansas Rifles could be swiftly brought up to support the Texans in their crossing. The strength of Rifles stemmed from the fact that the ford was in the centre of their regiment's patrol area, rather than concern over holding on to it.

Wanting to make his dash across the river with few if any casualties, Dusty had sent Red ahead to see if the Yankees were watching their rear. Trained in Indian warfare, Vern Hassle ran Kiowa a close second in ability. He had advanced to make a scout and his return heralded trouble.

"What's up?" Red demanded.

Before Hassle could reply, Red heard the staccato blast of a bugle blowing the "alarm." Faint shouts wafted back to the Texan's ears, followed by the crackle of rifle shots.

"That!" Hassle replied. "When I left, the Arkansas boys were forming up like they're fixing to attack the ford—and there's a battery of cannon on this side."

"Let's go!" Red barked. "Is anybody watching this way, Vern?"

"Nope," the corporal answered; then the four horses were running.

Urging their mounts to a gallop, Red's party raced across the remaining half mile and drew rein just before reaching the rim overlooking the Snake Ford. Dropping from his saddle, Red slid free the Henry rifle from its boot. Before leaving the horses ground-hitched, he told the others to take their carbines and ammunition. Thrusting a box of .44 bullets, taken from his saddle-pouch, into his tunic, Red advanced on foot until he could see the river.

The trail along which they had ridden wound down a gentle slope and across about a quarter of a mile of level ground before entering the water to emerge on the other bank which had the same general features. As the name implied, the Caddo made a S-shaped curve at that point. To either side of Red, the downwards slope extended until it eventually fell in a sheer wall to the water. There was, however, an area of about half a mile down which one could ride to reach the ford.

All that Red had expected to see from his study of the maps. What came as a shock was the sight of the Arkansas Rifles battalion formed up in line of battle and starting to advance determinedly down the opposite slope. That and the battery of Model 1857 12-pounder Napoleon gun-howitzers facing the Rebels on the Yankees' shore. From all appearances, the whole battalion, colours flying and bayonets fixed, were moving to the attack. Their numbers would have been adequate against the normal guard, even if the assault led to casualties from the enemies' rifle fire. The same did not apply when they must advance across more than eight hundred yards of open country, in the face of artillery bombardment, before reaching the river.

Red knew that a well-served Napoleon could fire two aimed shots a minute, using spherical case or solid shot. When the range shortened, the guns would switch to canister and speed up their rate of fire. Canister, each one holding twenty-seven balls, turned the Napoleons into a kind of giant shotgun and dispensed with the need for taking careful aim. It could not be put into use successfully until the enemy came within three hundred and fifty yards range; but after that every gun in the battery could get off up to nine shots before the attackers reached it. Such a volume of fire might easily wipe out the whole battalion.

Already solid shot was crashing among the advancing soldiers, the Yankee battery commander wisely forgetting spherical case due to the uncertainty of the timing-fuses' operation. Down by the river, the Zouaves and Dragoons crouched in their defensive positions and exchanged shots with the Rifles' skirmishers. So far the Yankee infantry did not fire at the main body of the attackers. Almost half a mile was not a distance over which the average soldier, armed with the U.S. Model of 1861 rifle-musket could be counted on to make a hit.

On marched the Arkansas Rifles, keeping their ranks well despite the canon-fire. In front strode the colour party, bearing the regiment's battle-flag, and officers with drawn swords. The enlisted men carried Enfield rifles at the high-port. It would be several mintues before they were close enough to put the rifles into effective use and all that time the Napoleons would continue to fire at them.

"We've got to stop those guns!" Red snapped.

"You mean for us four to charge down there and do it?" asked Tracey Prince.

"Just three of us," Red corrected. "Vern. Take my horse and ride relay to the Company. Tell Cap'n Fog what's coming off here."

"How about you?" the old corporal inquired.

"We're going to move down the rim, find places to settle in and start to shooting," Red explained. "Move it!"

"Yo!" replied Prince and Private Tarp Hayley eagerly, each holding a Sharps carbine. Like Red's Henry, the Sharps were battle-field captures and effective weapons in skilled hands.

Studying the battery as he and his companions passed over the rim, while Hassle hurried off to deliver the message, Red concluded that it had only recently arrived and come hurriedly. He could see no sign of the battery-wagon —which carried tents and suplies for the guns' crews—the travelling forage or six reserve caissons of ammunition which normally accompanied the Napoleons when they moved. While there had been some attempt to conceal the guns behind bushes, the crews had not raised protective earth-works. Nor had the three ammunition chests been removed from the guns' caissons and brought closer to the pieces. So far the crews had fed their guns with charges brought from the limber's chest. Their teams and the Dragons' horses were held among a clump of trees over by the left side wall.

"Fan out and find cover!" Red snapped to Hayley and Prince. "Don't bother with the Zouaves, go for the gun crews."

Swiftly they separated and each found a place which he felt suited his needs. Red flattened behind a rock, setting the box of bullets close to his left hand. Three hundred yards lay between him and the nearest cannon. The battery, spaced at around fourteen yards intervals and allowing a further two yards per gun, covered an eighty-two yards front. Which meant even the outer pieces were in range of his Henry or his companions' Sharps carbines.

Grimly Red set his rifle's sights. With the wind blowing towards the Confederate side of the ford, Dusty might not hear the fighting. That meant there would be a delay before help could come. So Red knew what must be done. Unless the guns' rate of fire was reduced, the Arkansas Rifles faced terrible losses. The bellowing of the Napoleons and sight of Confederate soldiers falling told him that.

Taking aim, Red squeezed the Henry's trigger and felt the recoil's kick against his shoulder. Through the swirling powder-smoke, he saw the chief-of-piece for the third gun from the left stagger and fall. Down and up flicked the Henry's lever, throwing an empty cartridge case into the air. Before it landed, Red had swung the barrel and shot the number-one man of the crew. Caught in the act of ramming a solid shot down the barrel, the soldier collapsed and snapped the shaft of the rammer. Until a spare could be brought up, the gun was out of action.

Swiftly Red changed his point of aim, raking the fourth from left gun with half-a-dozen bullets. He hit two men and threw the rest into such confusion that the piece went unfired. From the sound of carbine shots on either side of him, he knew that Prince and Hayley were doing their part in slowing the battery's' rate of fire.

Already the artillerymen were beginning to realize that the bullets did not come from the Arkansas Rifles and started to look for their new assailants. All too well they understood the danger to themselves. In the days of its greatest exponent, Napoleon Bonaparte, cannon-fire and especially canister had been a most deadly weapon to employ against unprotected bodies of troops. While canister was still terrible, improvements in hand-held arms had rendered it less effective and it no longer had the advantage of superior range over rifles. So the Yankees wanted to make the most of the canister before the Arkansas Rifles came too close.

Seeing his men go down, the major commanding the battery swung to look at the slope. In doing so, he inadver-

tently saved his life. Kneeling behind a rock some thirty
yards to Red's right, Hayley had selected the major as his
next mark. He touched off his shot just as the officer
moved and missed.

About the same disitance to Red's left, Prince rested his
carbine on the lip of the hollow in which he crouched,
sighted and fired. Caught in the head, the number-three
man of the far left cannon spun around and with a spas-
modic gesture flung away the vent-pick with which he had
been about to prick open the loaded serge powder bag to
make way for the insertion of the friction-primer. Cursing,
the chief-of-piece fumbled in his pockets for another vent-
pick, without which the gun could not be fired.

The major raked the slope with his field-glasses and
located his attackers. Only three men, but they posed a
serious threat to the battery's efficiency. Snapping an order
to his orderly, he sent the man racing with a message to the
Zouaves' commanding officer.

Watching the orderly, Red guessed at the nature of his
mission. Across the river, the Arkansas Rifles were still
marching at quick-time with their colonel striding in front
of them. Not until within a hundred yards would they make
their charge. The harassing of the Napoleons must continue
if the charge was to succeed.

Although his Henry still held five rounds, Red rested its
butt on the ground and began to reload. Opening the maga-
zine-tube after forcing its spring towards the muzzle, he
fed ten flat-nosed .44/28 bullets base first down the tube to
refill it. While working, he blessed the fact that he had
brought the Henry along instead of his Spencer—also a
battle-field capture. The Spencer might be more powerful,
but had a slower rate of fire and only a seven-shot magazine.

While Red reloaded the Henry, his companions' single-
shot carbines continued to crack. Clearly they were having
some effect, for the Napoleons' fire slackened.

"Bunch of Yankee puddle-splashers coming, Mr.
Blaze!" called Prince.

"Go for the battery as long as you can," Red replied,

closing the magazine tube and returning to his firing position.

A dozen Zouaves led by a sergeant ran by the guns towards the slopes, but they would have to be ignored until the last minute. Already the Arkansas Rifles had entered the zone in which canister could be used against them. Nor did they show signs of halting while rifle fire beat down the menace of the Napoleons.

With a grim-set face Red poured bullets at one of the centre guns. Watching men go down, he noticed that the piece at the left of the line stood unattended. Clearly he and his men had inflicted sufficient casualties for the battery's commander to concentrate the depleted crew on other guns.

Down below, a Springfield rifle banged. Its .58 calibre ball spattered rock chips from Red's cover. Changing his line of sight, the red head sprayed lead at the Zouaves. He dropped the sergeant and one man, then wounded another before the rest took cover. The speed at which he had fired warned the Yankees that they were facing a good shot armed with a Henry, fastest-shooting rifle of the War. So they flung themselves to shelter instead of carrying out their orders. Once more Red turned his attention to the Napoleons.

When the Texans continued to shoot at his guns, the major sent another message to the Zouave entrenchments. Red saw the Infantry major stare up the slope and hesitate, wanting to retain as many men as possible to meet the Rifles' onslaught. Yet he also saw the danger if the harassment of the battery continued. Its fire had already been reduced to a half and at a time when it should be at its highest. So he gave an order which sent a further twenty men under the command of a lieutenant towards the slope.

Seeing support on its way, the first party of Zouaves resumed their advance. Darting from cover to cover, they ascended the slope. Once again Red began to reload the Henry. Unnoticed by him, a Zouave rose from behind a bush and lined a long-barrelled rifle at him.

Catching a movement from the corner of his eye, Tracey

Prince turned his head to take a closer look. He saw the Zouave behind Red and twisted around to aim and fire his carbine. In doing so, he saved his and Red's lives. Even as he moved, another Zouave appeared and took a shot at him. The bullet spanged off the rock where Prince's body had been resting an instant before, but without affecting his accuracy. The Sharps spat and blood masked the face of the man beyond Red. Dropping his Springfield he turned and stumbled blindly down the slope.

On firing, Prince swung to face the threat to his own existence. Standing in plain sight, as the reloading could be done faster that way than when kneeling or prone, the second Zouave went about it with trained speed. Clearly he was a veteran, fully capable of making the best time possible at the tedious business of recharging the obsolete, muzzle-loading Springfield rifle. Already he had withdrawn a paper cartridge from his belt-pouch, torn open its base with his teeth, poured the powder into the barrel, used the covering as a wad and thrust the round ball into the muzzle. Resting the cup-shaped end of the ramrod on to the ball, he drove it to the bottom of the barrel. No less speedily he removed the rod, dropping it once clear of the muzzle, and drew back the hammer to half cock.

Although black powder fouled badly when discharged, firing one bullet did not build up sufficient residue to make thrusting home the next round a difficult process. So in slightly less than twenty seconds after missing Prince, the Zouave was ready to fit a percussion cap on the nipple and try again.

Unfortunately Prince held one of the weapons which rapidly wrote a finish to the cheap-to-produce, easy-to-maintain muzzle-loading rifles with which both sides had ben armed at the start of the War.

While turning, Prince had shoved forward the Sharps' trigger-guard. This in turn caused the breech block to descend into its loading position. Like the rifle, the carbine fired a non-metallic cartridge; but he did not have to bite it open. Slipping the bullet into the chamber, he returned the triggerguard to its normal place. As it closed, the knife-edge of the breech block sheared through the linen base of the cartridge. Nor did he need to fumble with percussion caps.

The Maynard-primer, which looked like and acted in the manner of a child's roller-cap pistol, had failed to meet the stringent demands of war. Amongst its other faults, the allegedly waterproof coating had allowed the patches of fulminate to become damp and inoperative. So the United States Army had gone back to the slower, but more certain, individual copper cap for the Springfield. The Sharps used the simple, effective Lawrence disc-primer. Operated by a spring-fed magazine built into the frame, the primer fed percussion discs on to the nipple of the carbine's breech and utilized the falling hammer to place them there as well as igniting the fulminate. In that way, the Lawrence primer did away with capping by hand and increased the Sharps' rate of fire.

Making a snap alignment of the sights, Prince squeezed the trigger. The .52 calibre Sharps bullet tore into the Zouave as he was taking a percussion cap from its box. Twisting around, he fell back out of the Texan's sight.

Hayley set his sights on the number-six man as he lifted a round of canister from the limber of the gun on the right of the battery. Engrossed in his work, the Texan forgot to stay alert. As his carbine cracked, three rifles banged like an echo. All three bullets found their billet in Hayley's body and he died without witnessing the excellent result of his last shot. The sort-barrelled Sharps carbine lacked the extreme long-range accuracy of the Company's excellent rifles. At ranges of around three hundred yards, the impact point of the bullet might vary by several inches no matter how carefully it had been aimed. Flying down the slope, Hayley's lead ploughed through the round's paper covering and into the serge bag of black powder. Ignited by the heat of the bullet, the two-and-a-half pound charge exploded. Caught in the blast, the remaining charges in the limber detonated. The numbers five, six and seven crew members disappeared in a flash of raging light and roar of sound. Flung from their feet, the remainder of the gun's crew and

of the neighbouring piece stayed down until sure that there
would be no sympathetic explosion from the next limber's
chest.

After shooting Hayley, the three Zouaves hurled themselves into the nearest cover. They had seen enough of the
Texans' deadly shooting not to risk standing exposed while
reloading their rifles. Others of their party continued to
advance. In the lead, the young lieutenant made for Red's
position with his sword in the right hand and revolver in
the left.

Pumping lead through the red-hot barrel of his Henry,
Red was momentarily dazed by the limber's disintegration.
Across the river the Arkansas Rifles were wavering under
the hammering of the Napoleons, reduced though it had
been. They also faced the volley-firing of the Zouaves and
Dragoons. So Red ignored the danger to himself and concentrated on getting off as many aimed shots as he could at
the battery.

CHAPTER SIX

Yeeah, Texas Light!

Even as Red worked the Henry's lever and tried to remember how many bullets he had fired since last replenishing the magazine, he heard the wild, ringing notes of a bugle blowing the "charge." Twisting his head involuntarily towards the sound, he saw Dusty galloping over the rim, followed by most of the Company.

A revolver barked close at hand, its bullet tearing the hat from Red's head. That brought his attention to more pressing matters than admiring his companions' riding skill, or blessing his cousin's timely arrival. Swinging to face the direction from which the shot had come, he saw the Yankee lieutenant looming towards him. Again the Zouave's revolver spat. Its bullet struck the barrel of the Henry and spun it from Red's hands. With a yell of triumph, the Zouave sprang forward and swung up the sword. Red threw himself to one side, right hand turning palm-out to close on the butt of the off-side Colt. Fetching it from leather as he landed on his back, he fired upwards. Caught under the chin by the bullet, the Yankee officer staggered into the path of one of his men who was trying to draw a bead on Red. Thwarted in his attempt and seeing the Rebel cavalry rushing down the slope, the soldier dropped his rifle and fled.

Knowing that he could not join in the charge while afoot, Red holstered his Colt and rolled across to pick up the Henry. He found that the bullet had only glanced off the top of the octagonal barrel. Satisfied that the rifle was operative, he turned his eyes towards the battery once more.

On hearing Hassle's news, Dusty had wasted no time. Signalling in the flanking pickets to increase his fighting-strength, he had left Sergeant Weather and six reluctant men to control the captured horses and brought up the rest as fast as he could. By the time he reached the rim, he had been prepared to launch an immediate attack. Many Confederate cavalry regiments placed their assault emphasis on firearms, but the Texas Light Cavalry always made use of their sabres in a charge. So every man had his reins fastened to the saddlehorn, guiding his horse with his knees while holding a sabre in one hand and revolver in the other.

"Yeeah, Texas Light!"

Loud rang the Texans' battle-shout, mingling with the bugler's spirited rendition of the "charge," sounding above the drumming of over fifty sets of thundering hooves. Forming a single line parallel to the river, the grey-clad riders urged their horses on with wild, grim determination.

Becoming aware of the new peril, the crew of the number three gun sprang to its trail-bar. Under the profane urgings of the chief-of-piece and battery commander, they lifted the stock of the gun and started to drag its 2332 pounds of tube and carriage around to face the Texans. Red and Prince saw what was planned and turned their weapons towards the gun. Under the combined hail of fire, three men fell and the remainder were prevented from bringing the piece to bear on Company "C."

Taking heart at the sight of the cavalry, the Arkansas Rifles raised a cheer. Their line, faltering before the depleted battery's canister, straightened and pressed forward. From a hesitant walk, they swung back into quick-time and built up to a double march into the shallow water of the ford. Down went the bearer of the regimental colour, shot by a Zouave. Although badly wounded, he kept the flag held in the air until another member of the colour guard took it from his hand. Having done his duty, the stricken man collapsed and lay still.

Even as Dusty led his men down the slope, he wondered what had caused such an attack to be launched on the ford. It could be part of some new offensive planned by Ole

Devil after Company "C" had left on their current mission. Yet he doubted if his uncle would permit an unsupported assault.

Not that Dusty devoted much time to idle conjecture. Although Red and Prince had prevented the turning of the Napoleon, Company "C" did not ride unchallenged. Some of the Zouaves and Dragoons had turned from the advancing Rifles and opened fire on the approaching cavalry. A cry of pain from behind him told Dusty that at least one of the bullets had taken effect.

The ground shook and trembled to the thundering hooves. Best mounted of the Texans, Dusty had drawn slightly ahead of the Company. Suddenly he felt a sharp jolt run through his racing horse and knew what it meant. The big black horse—one of three he had broken and trained—screamed, staggered and started to go down with a bullet in its chest. Instantly Dusty kicked his feet from the stirrups, tossing his right leg up and across the saddle. As the horse crumpled forward, he sprang from its back. His momentum carried him clear, but he was in danger of being ridden down by the rushing men behind him.

Looking back, he saw a riderless horse approaching in the lead of the Company. Twirling away the revolver, he sprang forward to catch hold of the empty saddle's horn and vaulted astride. The leather was slick with the previous user's blood, but he retained his seat and charged onwards. Without any conscious thought on his part, he drew the revolver ready for use.

Springing away from the half-turned gun, the sergeant chief-of-piece rushed at Dusty and lashed out with his short artillery sword. Down flickered the small Texan's Haiman sabre, catching and deflecting the Yankee's blade. Then Dusty lunged, driving his point into the man's chest and dragging it free as the horse carried him by. A revolver crashed from the left, its bullet fanning the air by Dusty's face. Almost of its own volition, the bone-handled Army Colt lined and barked an answer. Hit between the eyes, the battery commander let his smoking revolver drop and followed it to the ground. Hardly aware of having shot the

Yankee major, Dusty whirled his horse in a rearing, sliding turn to see where he could best direct his activities.

As always under such conditions, Dusty later remembered only flashes of what followed, brief, flickering cameos from the bloody fight raging on the Snake Ford of the Caddo. While shooting the Yankee major, he saw that the Arkansas Rifles had crossed the river and were engaging the defenders with bayonets. Bodies lay in the water and the down-stream current was tinged a pinkish-red with their blood.

Not far from Dusty, charging forward with his Enfield and bayonet at the ready, an Arkansas Rifles private made for a terrified Zouave drummer-boy. Letting his bugle fall, the boy sank to his knees. At the last moment, the soldier swerved and left the boy kneeling unharmed, with eyes closed and lips moving in a soundless prayer.

An artilleryman lined his revolver at one of the passing Texans. Before he could press the trigger, he was knocked sprawling by Billy Jack's horse. He was not given a chance to recover. Rushing up, the Rebel who had spared the drummer-boy plunged home the bayonet and pinned him to the ground.

One of the Napoleons roared, hurling its charge of canister indiscriminately into the wild hacking, thrusting scrimmage of Yankees and Rebels before it. Blue- and grey-uniformed bodies tumbled together, torn open by the flying 1.5 inch balls from the cannon. Reining his horse alongside it, a Texas sprang from his saddle. He landed on the tube, miraculously keeping his balance while kicking one of the crew in the face and cutting down the chief-of-piece with his sabre. Then he pitched sideways, shot by the lieutenant who commanded the two-piece section to which the gun belonged. An instant later the officer also lay dead, shot in the back of the head by an Enfield bullet.

Sweeping away from the rest of the Company, Vern Hassle and six men descended on the four Yankees who had been detailed to watch over the artillery's and Dragoons' picketed horses. One of the Union soldiers tried to fight. Without slowing his horse, Hassle cut loose with his

old Dragoon Colt. He hit the man and hurled him backwards. Another of the horse-minders went down before the
last two threw aside their unfired carbines and raised their
hands in surrender. Leaving half of his party to deal with
the prisoners, Hassle set the others to work calming the
Yankee horses and preventing any from tearing free and
escaping.

On the edge of the trenches, the Arkansas Rifles' tall,
lean colonel and the major commanding the Zouaves
fought a savage duel with their swords. Seeing his chance,
Colonel Barnett went into a near-classic lunge and spiked
his point between the other's ribs. Behind the colonel, a
Dragoon sergeant flung up and lined his carbine. Charging
in, a mounted Texan almost severed the Yankee non-com's
head from his shoulders before he could fire.

As the fight ebbed his way, an artillery lieutenant sprang
on to a caisson and jerked up the lid of the forward chest.
Drawing his revolver, he pointed it downwards. A fanatical
Unionist, he intended to take as many of the hated Rebels
with him as he could, without regard for his own men who
would also perish. Reining his borrowed mount around,
Dusty raised his Colt shoulder high. Sighting on the Yankee officer, he fired—and not a moment too soon. Rocked
backwards by the .44 ball, the lieutenant got off his shot.
The bullet flung up splinters from the edge of the chest, but
did not hit and explode the charges inside it.

Then the fight was over. Assailed from two sides, left
virtually leaderless the Yankees discarded their rifles or
carbines. Hands shot into the air and yells of surrender
rang out. Despite the growing trend in the East towards
Southern defeat, the Confederate States' Army of Arkansas
had scored another victory on the bloody banks of the
Caddo River.

Returning his Colt to its holster, Dusty rode towards
where the Arkansas Rifles' colonel stood glaring around.
Instead of showing pleasure, or gratitude for Company
"C"'s assistance, Colonel Harvey Barnett eyed Dusty with
every indication of fury.

"Where the hell have you been, damn you?" Barnett roared as Dusty swung from his saddle.

A slight frown creased the small Texan's face at the furious greeting. After bringing his men on to the scene at such an opportune moment, he felt that he deserved a more civil and reasonable response. Any commanding officer would be shaken after suffering heavy losses, but Barnett's attitude hinted at more than that. From the way he had spoken, it almost seemed that he not only expected Company "C" to arrive but felt they should have come earlier in the attack.

"Raiding across the Ouachita, sir," Dusty answered holding his temper in check and sticking the point of his sabre into the ground to leave his hands free.

"Raiding!" Barnett blazed, face almost white with rage. Then, with a visible effort, he regained control of his emotions. "I'll speak to you when I've attended to my duties, Captain Fog. And you'd be advised to see to your own."

"Yo!" Dusty answered saluting.

Wondering what had caused the colonel to act in such a strange manner, Dusty saw Sandy McGraw approaching. He told the guidon-carrier to retrieve his saddle from the dead horse and handed over his sabre. Walking to rejoin his men, he saw Red and Prince standing on the slope looking at the still shape of Tarp Hayley.

"What in hell're them puddle-splashers doing, Cap'n Dusty?" Billy Jack demanded, coming over. "They could've got wiped out, attacking that way, if we hadn't happened along."

"Sure," Dusty replied. "Secure the prisoners, see to the wounded, put pickets on the rim to watch for Yankee reinforcements."

"Yo!" Billy Jack answered.

Half an hour went by and Dusty's orders were well on their way to completion. Red had just returned to report that the Company had lost six dead and eight wounded when Dusty saw Barnett and the Rifles' stocky, middle-aged adjutant, 1st Lieutenant le Branche, approaching. Before they reached the young Texans, the two officers halted and stared up the slope. Having heard no warning from the pickets he had put out, Dusty turned to learn what attracted their attention. He saw Kiowa and Weather driving the captured remounts and draught horses down the slope. Facing Barnett, Dusty found that the expression of anger had returned to the colonel's features and felt surprised at the reaction. He could not see why the evidence of a successful raid should bring such a response.

"Where did you get those horses?" Barnett demanded, gritting out the words.

"I took most of them from the Yankees out by Lake Ouachita, sir."

"You mean that you have the audacity to admit you went off on a raiding mission without first reporting yourself to *me?*"

"I beg your pardon, sir?" Dusty said, completely baffled by the comment.

The Texas Light Cavalry rarely received orders to report to a ford's guard before entering Yankee territory. On his present assignment, Dusty had not even made his crossing anywhere near the Snake Ford.

"Damn it, Fog! You're not deaf and don't act the innocent with me!" Barnett raged. "Were you, or were you not under orders to give my battalion a cavalry screen and support during the attack on this ford?"

"I was not, sir!" Dusty stated flatly.

Soften-spoken the reply might have been, but it held a ring of truth. Barnett stiffened, staring hard at Dusty's face.

"If you weren't, then who was?" the colonel growled. "And where the hell are they now?"

"I couldn't say, sir. I've been over the Ouachita for six days on a general reconnaisance and raiding mission. It's only by chance that I came back this way and I've seen no sign of any other cavalry unit."

Being aware, and mostly approving, of Ole Devil Hardin's policy of sending cavalry raiders across the Ouachita, Barnett thought of his own losses and his anger did not lessen. However he no longer blamed Dusty for his misfortune or the failure of the cavalry cover to arrive. At first, and more so when he had seen the captured horses on the rim, Barnett had suspected that Dusty was sent to support him but had crossed the river on a self-appointed raiding mission.

"My apologies, Captain Fog," Barnett said. "I see you aren't at fault. In fact if your men hadn't harassed the battery my losses would have been far heavier!"

"That was Mr. Blaze's work, sir," Dusty corrected.

"I'll see that you're commended for it, Mr. Blaze," Barnett promised, then frowned and went on, "This whole damned affair's been bungled somewhere."

"How's that, sir?" Dusty asked.

"This morning I received orders from General Hardin to take this ford by noon today."

"Why, sir?"

"As a crossing for our troops when we commence an offensive tomorrow."

Instead of clarifying the matter, the words merely increased Dusty's mystification. Only the day before he had left on the patrol, he had overheard Ole Devil angrily damning the shortage of men and materials which prevented the Army of Arkansas from taking more effective measures against the Yankees. Of course, in six days the situation could have changed. While there had hardly been time for reinforcements to arrive, Ole Devil might be under orders to start a campaign designed to draw Union troops away from the hard-pressed Southern armies in the east.

Yet, knowing his uncle, Dusty doubted if he would order an infantry attack—even by a battalion against the normal company and platoon guard of the Yankees—without ensuring it had the backing of cavalry. Ole Devil did not squander his men's lives in such a reckless manner. Which brought up another point. The Snake Ford was far from an ideal place from which to launch an offensive. Usually the Yankees felt it so unimportant that they maintained only a small guard. It might be no more than coincidence that they had strengthened the defences—or there could be another, more sinister reason.

"When did the battery move in, sir?" Dusty inquired.

"Last night. I must admit that it came as a shock to see them in position, especially when I received the order to attack. If it had come from anybody but Ole Devil, I'd have hesitated to obey without having seen the cavalry—"

"How did the order come, sir?" Dusty wanted to know, for the gist of the colonel's words struck him as significant.

"In the usual way," le Branche answered for Barnett. "By a Texas Light Cavalry courier."

"You accepted it, mister?" Dusty asked.

"Of course."

"Did you know the courier?"

"I don't recall having seen him before, the adjutant admitted. "But they change regularly and he acted in the normal way."

"Which doesn't mean to say he was genuine," Dusty pointed out.

Every instinct the small Texan possessed warned him that there was something very wrong with the orders. The possibility of an imposter delivering fakes was not wildly unlikely. Even if the Yankees did not have Texas Light Cavalry uniforms taken from corpses or prisoners, their tailors could easily make one. Both Union and Confederate officers had received their earliest training before the War in the U.S. Military Academy at West Point. The drill, organization and ceremonial of the C.S.A. for the most part copied that of the Union. Some Texans had elected to serve the North when their State seceded. So if an imposter delivered false orders, he would not only dress correctly and know the routine, but could also talk like a loyal son of the Lone Star State.

"Are you saying there's something wrong with that order, Captain?" asked Barnett.

"It's just a hunch, sir," Dusty replied. "Those Napoleons happened along at a mighty convenient time and the cavalry support you expected never came."

Opening the sabretasche suspended from his left shoulder, le Branche drew out several sheets of paper and held the top one to Dusty saying, "This is it."

At first glance, and on closer inspection, the order appeared to be genuine. The type of paper used, the printed heading, even the phrasing of the various commands and instructions were faultless. So Dusty looked long and hard at the signature on the bottom.

"This's not General Hardin's writing, sir," he finally told Barnett. "It's a real good copy, but that's all it is."

CHAPTER SEVEN

It's Our Turn to Play Tricky

Taking the sheet of paper from Dusty's hand, Barnett compared it with other orders which he knew to be genuine. At last the colonel nodded grimly and admitted that it was a cleverly-contrived fake. Nor did he need to strain his brain to decide what lay behind its production and delivery. Morale was high amongst the Confederate troops in Arkansas and they had complete faith in their commanding general.

As Barnett had been about to say earlier, he would have hesitated to make the attack when his cavalry screen had failed to announce its presence if the order had come from anybody other than Ole Devil Hardin. The forged document promised that the horse-soldiers would be in position and that, backed by Ole Devil's signature, had been sufficient for the colonel.

Expecting the cavalry support promised by their respected general, even though they had not seen it, the men of the Arkansas Rifles' battalion had marched on the ford in the face of the newly-arrived Yankee battery. They might easily have been decimated by the Napoleons. Meeting with a crushing defeat would have shattered the survivors' faith in Ole Devil and the mistrust would have spread through the rest of the Confederate Army under his command. The bloody repulse would also have done much to boost the flagging spirits of the Union Army opposing them.

Which brought up another point—one shocking to its implications. Dusty saw it first, expressing it even as it started to form among his companions.

"Likely the Yankees wouldn't send out just one set of orders!"

A shocked silence followed Dusty's words. The colonel and two lieutenants exchanged apprehensive looks. Perhaps at that moment along the Caddo and Ouachita Rivers other Confederate soldiers were marching gallantly to their deaths, expecting help which would not come.

"Red!" Dusty went on, knowing there was no telegraph communication between the Caddo and Upper Ouachita fords. "Pick relays of good horses for you, Billy Jack, Kiowa and Vern Hassle. Two of you'll go down-river, two up, as fast as you can push three horses. Warn every ford guard and patrol you come across not to make an attack if they've just had orders to do it."

"It'll be too late!" le Branche protested. "That damned son-of-a-bitch left almost four hours ago."

"We've still got to try," Dusty replied. "How many horses had he?"

"Just the one," le Branche answered. "And he went downriver."

"We might catch up with him," Red decided. "I'll see if the Yankees've enough good horses along, Cou—Cap'n."

"Do that," Dusty confirmed and turned to Barnett. "Our own mounts've been hard-pushed these last few days, sir."

"I understand," the colonel replied and a frosty smile played briefly on his lips. "Horses aren't like infantrymen, they get tired after a few miles. Use my name as your authority for countermanding the orders, Mr. Blaze."

"Yo!" Red replied, saluting and swinging on his heel to stride away.

The surviving company commanders of the battalion approached their colonel. Not knowing that the order had been a fake, they scowled at Dusty. Before any of them could speak, Barnett gave them the order to withdraw to their own lines.

"With the colonel's permission—?" Dusty put in.

"What is it, Captain Fog?" Barnett asked, then told le Branche to explain to the three majors why the cavalry support had been delayed in its arrival.

"Why don't we hold this side of the river now we've taken it, sir?" Dusty suggested ignoring the comments which followed le Branche's explanation.

"I've had heavy losses—"

"My Company's at your disposal until reinforcements arrive, sir," Dusty offered. "And enough of them know how to handle a cannon for us to make use of those captured Napoleons. It could be that our Army'll need something to hold the Yankees' attention for a spell."

"Keep talking," Barnett prompted.

"With the start he's got, my men aren't likely to catch that feller in time to stop the attacks. After the losses they'll suffer, the ford guards won't be in any shape to fight off determined counter-attacks—"

"That's true," admitted the colonel and his majors rumbled their agreement.

"So I reckon we should make ready to hold that rim up there," Dusty continued. "And make sure the Yankees know that's what we're fixing to do."

"How do we do that?" asked le Branche.

"By turning loose all the prisoners, including the wounded. I'll have some of my boys make up Indian-style litters for them. Among the horses we give the Yankees to haul the litters, there'll be a fast saddle-mount—by accident, of course."

"And one of the officers we free'll use it to find the nearest Yankee force and tell them what's happening here," Barnett finished as Dusty paused for breath. "With luck they'll come for us instead of attacking the other fords. That'll give Old Devil time to rush up reinforcements."

"That's assuming the order's a fake and this's a plot," put in the major commanding Company "E," which had suffered heaviest in the attack.

"You've my word that that's not General Hardin's signature sir," Dusty answered politely. "And the whole deal strikes me as the kind of tricky play the new Yankee general would make. I've come across another example of it with these remounts I captured at the top end of Lake Hamilton. Their escort was carrying a fake document."

"Buller'd never've been smart enough to think of it, that's for sure," Barnett growled. "And a series of victories brought about by Trumpeter would set his command off to a good start."

"Yes, sir, it would," Dusty agreed. "Which's one of the reasons why I reckon we should make them fight hard to retake this side of the river, even if he doesn't aim to use the orders as openers in an offensive. That way his men won't think his notion was so all-fired smart after all."

"They sure as hell won't," enthused Barnett. "Damned if we don't give it a whirl, gentlemen."

"There's another thing, sir—" Dusty began.

"Tell us, Cap'n Fog. You've made right good sense so far."

"I reckon it's our turn to play tricky. Let's make the fellers we turn loose think that we knew all along the order was a fake, but went along with it so's we could spring our own trap and capture the battery."

"By cracky, yes!" boomed Barnett. "They'll blame Trumpeter all the more that way. And, thinking of their own losses, they'll be more likely to overlook how many we had killed. See to the arrangements, gentlemen. Captain Fog, have a man with a fast horse ready to deliver our reports to General Hardin. My own couriers both went to have their horses re-shod this morning before the messenger arrived with that order and aren't back yet. Your man can call in at my regimental headquarters and I'll ask for some help to be sent in."

"Yo!" Dusty replied, then stiffened to a brace and continued, "Could your men be told what's happened, sir? That way they won't go to blaming my boys for us not showing up earlier in the attack."

Barnett sucked in a deep breath, knowing that to follow Dusty's request would mean admitting that he had been taken for a sucker. Yet not to do so might bring trouble in its wake. So he nodded and agreed to pass on the facts to his men. Once that was done, he could only hope that he would redeem himself by making a success of defending the captured strip of territory.

Holding their horses to a fast, mile-devouring half-gallop, Red Blaze and Kiowa followed the trail through the wooded country alongside the Caddo River. They had been fortunate in finding eight Dragoon horses suitable for their mission. It had been decided that Red and Kiowa should head down-river, while Billy Jack and Vern Hassle would carry the warning in the other direction. Behind them, Dusty's plan was already being put into action. They hoped that it would succeed, or Trumpeter's boast of conquering Texas might yet be fulfilled.

All the time they rode, Kiowa kept his eyes darting from side to side. He studied the river's bank with care, but also gave attention to the thick cover on the other side of the trail. They did not meet up with a Confederate patrol, but that was no surprise. The Arkansas Rifles battalion supplied the patrols along that stretch of the river and Barnett had not sent any out after receiving the order to make the attack.

Soon after passing the confluence of the Caddo and Ouachita Rivers, Kiowa brought his two-horse relay to a sudden halt. Reining in his own mounts, Red watched the sergeant drop to the ground and plunge into the bushes lining the river-side of the trail. Wondering what had attracted Kiowa's attention, Red prepared to follow him. Before he could do so, Red had to make a grab at and catch the reins of the sergeant's horses. Unlike Kiowa's usual mounts, the animals acquired from the Dragoons had not been trained to stand ground-hitched and showed signs of continuing along the path.

"What's up, Kiowa?" Red called, impatiently curbing the restless fiddle-footing of the four horses.

"Saw something that looked powerful like a feller's leg in here," the scout answered. "And it is one."

Swinging from his saddle, Red took the precaution of securing the relays' reins to the branches of a sturdy bush. Then he went to join Kiowa and found the sergeant looking down at a body. It was bare-foot, unarmed, with the linings of its pockets turned inside out. Clad in the uniform of a Texas Light Cavalry private, the corpse had two bullets in its back to tell the cause of death. Bending forward, Kiowa rolled the body over and they studied its agony-distorted features.

"I can't mind him," the scout commented. "Which I ain't claiming to know every feller in the outfit."

"He's not one of the regular couriers, that's for sure," Ree replied. "This looks like border-jumpers' work, Kiowa."

"Sure enough does. Ain't nobody but a bunch of murdering guerillas'd take a man's boots and turn out his pockets after they've killed him. You want for me to take out after 'em, Mr. Blaze? They're headed for the river."

"They'll be across it by now," Red replied and made a wry face. "I'd best see if he's got anything left to tell us who he is."

While Red went about the distasteful task of searching the body, Kiowa made a thorough examination of the area. The Indian-dark sergeant paid great attention to the age of the various tracks and formed his conclusions.

"Anything?" Kiowa asked as Red straightened up.

"Nope. We'd best get on our way."

"Yep," Kiowa agreed. "Only there's likely no rush any more. He was killed 'tween three 'n' four hours back. Which means he's likely the son-of-a-bitch with the fake orders. You allowed he'd come down this way."

"Sure I did, and the time'd be about right," Red replied, covering the dead face with his bandana. "Only we daren't count on it being him. Let's ride. We'll have the next ford's guard send somebody out for him."

Returning to their horses, they freed the reins, mounted and continued with their assignment. While certain that Kiowa had formed a correct estimation of when the man was killed, Red kept them moving at a fast pace. It appeared likely that the imposter with the forged orders had fallen victim to a band of Yankee guerillas, a fate met by more than one lone man riding dispatch. In which case there would be no more unsupported attacks—unless there should be more than one man delivering the forgeries. Red figured he would rather be sure than sorry.

At last the Texans came into sight of the next ford and reined their horses to a stop. Studying the peaceful conditions which prevailed, Red let out a long sigh of relief. He could see no signs to tell that a battle had taken place recently. In fact from the lack of hostile action on the part of the rival guards, they might have been members of the same regiment camped for some reason on the opposite banks of the river.

Keen-eyed as always, Kiowa raked the Yankee's shore and spotted something which he regarded as significant despite the peaceful scene.

"I'll bet it was the feller with the false orders we found back there," the sergeant said. "There're half-a-dozen Napoleons hidden over that side and pointed this way."

Following the directions indicated by his companion, Red located one after another of the carefully-concealed cannon amongst the bushes. They were positioned so that their fire would effectively sweep the crossing.

"No bet," Red decided and starting his horse moving.

Riding into the Confederate camp, Red reported to the major commanding the guard. After hearing what had happened at the Snake Ford, the major said that the Napoleons had moved into position the previous night. He had received no orders to attack and nodded his agreement with Colonel Barnett's instructions that he ignore them should they arrive. Arranging for the body to be brought in as soon as possible, Red looked across the river.

"If that feller'd got here—" Red breathed.

"Yes," the major replied. "It's just what you'd expect a stinking Yankee soft-shell* to try and pull."

"Sure it is," Red drawled. *"After* he's tried to pull it."

Continuing their fast-paced journey, Red and Kiowa made for the next ford. On arrival, they found similar conditions to those at their last point of call. A battery of six-pounder cannon had been brought up the previous

*Soft-shell: a liberal-intellectual.

night, the pieces being concealed, yet able to lay a cross-fire on the ford. Until he had heard Red's news, the guard commander was at a loss to explain why the cannons had made their appearance. At first he had kept his men stood-to in their defensive positions, which explained why the Texans had not met a patrol between the two fords. The Union attack feared by the guard commander had not materialized and he had been on the point of sending a patrol along the river's bank when Red and Kiowa came on the scene. Repeating Colonel Barnett's orders, Red took to his horse once more.

After covering about a mile, the Texans met an infantry patrol travelling towards the ford they had just visited. Halting, Red learned that no orders to attack had been received by the next guard down-river; although it too was now covered by a battery of six-pounders. There had been no reports of trouble, or even artillery movements, from the lower fords. Learning of the incident at the Snake Ford, the infantry lieutenant stated his intention to watch extra carefully for fake couriers. Red warned him to make sure the courier was a fake and, if possible to take him alive.

"I'd sure hate the puddle-splashers to shoot down one of our boys who's riding dispatch, Kiowa," Red said as they watched the patrol march away. "There's no need to keep going."

"We headed back to the Company?" the sergeant inquired.

"Not by what you'd call the quickest way," Red answered. "I've been thinking about what Cousin Dusty's trying to do—"

"And?"

"The Yankee'll have at least three batteries against our one—soon's they can get the guns from the other fords to the Snake. Which they couldn't do happen somehow they was to lose all their hosses in the night."

"They do say Yankees are *real* careless with their stock," Kiowa grunted and fingered the knife on his belt. "We could go see if it's true."

"That's just what we'll do," Red decided; then a thought struck him and caused a grin to flicker across his face. "Wouldn't it be a pistol if those guerillas take them fake orders to sell to the Yankee soldiers? I'd give money to see old Trumpeter's face, happen he thought up this fancy twirl-me-round, when he gets his own orders handed back to him."

CHAPTER EIGHT

Your Guerilla Friend Killed One of Our Spies

Being a man who enjoyed his creature comforts, the Yankee general who had originally captured Little Rock selected a fine old colonial-style house in the best section of the town for his official residence. Ever optimistic, subsequent generals saw no point of seeking other quarters when at any time they might be continuing their advance towards the borders of Texas.

On the afternoon of the fourth day after his grand review had been disrupted and ruined, General Horace Trumpeter paced restlessly about the first-floor front room which had been converted into his private office. Back and forwards he tramped; from the door, passing the large desk in the centre of the room and almost brushing against the drawn-back, heavy drapes of the window in turning. Once he came to a halt by the window, glowering across the balcony into the foliage of the fine old white-oak tree which spread so close to the balustrade. The sight of the tree and the well-kept gardens stretching to the high walls surrounding the property gave him no pleasure that day. Scowling across the lawns and flower-beds, literally dotted and lined with decorative bushes, he gave an angry snort, then resumed his walking and thinking.

Normally his thoughts would have been directed to the future, planning the country that he intended to build after the War ended. It would be a fine country, where all men were equal—guided and directed, of course, by himself and a carefully selected few of the liberal elite—and worked for the common good. In his day-dreams, he could image himself as President, respected by all, receiving the adulation of the masses as the saviour of the Union and creator of a land which was "all for the people." They were the dreams first formed as a college student and the War had presented him with an opportunity to bring them to fulfillment.

Such thoughts did not wing their delightful way that afternoon. In tune with his thudding feet, two words repeatedly throbbed inside his head. "Dusty Fog! Dusty Fog! Dusty Fog!" Even before he had come to Arkanses, Trumpeter had heard the name. He had been one of those who raised their voices in protest against the Texan being permitted to attend and give evidence at Kirby Cogshill's court martial.* For the most part, Trumpeter had put the tales of Dusty Fog's abilities and talents down to nothing more than propaganda by the Confederate States. Trumpeter knew that he could not perform the feats credited to the Texan; which meant that no lesser mortal could do them. Since his arrival in Arkansas, he had seen evidence which would have caused a less egotistical man to change his mind.

The previous night Hoffinger had returned, bringing the news that the first consignment of remounts had fallen into enemy hands. That had been bad enough, but more so when Trumpeter's brilliant scheme to outwit the stupid Rebels had failed so badly. Far worse had been the discovery that the peckerwood† responsible for the loss was the same man who ruined the review.

Thinking back to the difficulties he had experienced in obtaining the money to purchase the remounts, Trumpeter cursed Dusty Fog's name. There would be career officers in plenty willing to crow "I told you so" when the news of the failure went the rounds. Feeling the pinch financially, Congress would display an even greater reluctance to hand out money that might be put to more spectacular, vote-catching use on the important, successful battle fronts.

No matter how he looked at recent events, Trumpeter could see only one bright spot. Brilliantly conceived, his plan for ruining the morale of Ole Devil Hardin's troops

---

*How Cogshill repaid Dusty is told in *Cuchilo*.

†Peckerwood: derogatory name for a white Southerner.

would still carry him through and win the acclaim he desired. Four assaults halted with heavy losses to the Rebels would make impressive reading in the Northern newspapers. More so when it would be remembered, pointed out even by a reporter-friend who had followed him to Little Rock, that before his arrival the Union's Army of Arkansas had known little other than continual defeat.

With the exception of ordering the batteries to the selected fords, the plan had been made and partially implemented before Trumpeter left Washington. Nor had he taken any of his new subordinates into his confidence. Only he and the trusted agent with the forged orders knew of the plan. While Trumpeter told himself that his reticence stemmed from caution and fear of discovery by the Rebel's efficient Secret Service, he knew it was because he wanted to be sure of success before announcing that the scheme had been tired.

So, knowing no better, the guards on the fords would regard the opportune arrival of the artillery as proof that their new general could out-think and out-plan the enemy. Such a belief in his omniscience would be of the greatest use in building up his troops' confidence, and holding it until the time came when he could make public the story of how he had tricked the Rebels and paved the way for the conquest of first Arkansas, then Texas.

Glancing out of the window in the course of his perambulations, he saw something which jolted him from his day-dreams. A smirk of triumph twisted at his lips as he came to a halt. Accompanied by a dishevelled, travel-stained 1st lieutenant, Colonel Verncombe came through the front gates. Anticipation tingled through Trumpeter as he watched the sentries break off their salutes to the visiting officers. Having expected reports of the repulses to arrive since noon, he decided that Verncombe must be bringing the first. Probably Verncombe wanted to deliver his congratulations in person. That, from a career soldier, would be a most satisfactory tribute.

Crossing to his desk, Trumpeter forced himself to sit down and assume a calm, passive appearance. When Vercombe arrived, the general wanted him to suspect nothing. That way, the approbation for showing the forethought to reinforce the fords' guard with artillery would be so much more pleasing. Time seemed to drag as he waited. At last he heard feet thudding on the passage beyond the door and he looked down at the papers on the desk. Without raising his head, he called, "Come in" when a knock sounded. His aide, a tall, slim lieutenant, entered to say that Colonel Verncombe requested an interview.

On being brought into Trumpeter's presence, Verncombe got straight down to business. Almost as soon as he had completed his salute, he started speaking and the words were not in the form of congratulations.

"Did you arrange for fake orders to be delivered to the Rebels on the Snake Ford of the Caddo—general?"

Something in the colonel's tone rang a warning bell in Trumpeter's head. Raising his eyes, he scowled at Verncombe's coldly angry face until the other belatedly added the final word. While Trumpeter rarely remembered military courtesy to his superiors, he expected it blindly and at all times from his juniors. Failing to stare down the Dragoon colonel, Trumpeter stiffened in his chair.

"I don't understand your question, colonel," Trumpeter said and his voice held a warning.

"It's simple enough—sir," Verncombe replied, too old a hand to permit his anger to lead him to indiscretion. "Did the general arrange for false orders to be delivered to the Rebels, causing them to make an assault on our guard at the Caddo River's Snake Ford—sir?"

"What makes you think I did?" Trumpeter demanded cautiously, guessing that something had gone wrong and determined to avoid making any statement which might lay the blame where it belonged, on him.

"Yesterday the Arkansas Rifles launched an attack on the ford and, despite a battery of our artillery having been moved in, took it from us."

"Took it?" The words burst from Trumpeter's lips before he could stop them.

"Yes—sir. The attack was made at battalion strength and with cavalry cover from our side of the river."

"And then what happened?" the general gritted.

"The guard on the ford and battery of Napoleons were captured," Verncombe told him, "after suffering heavy losses."

Wanting a scapegoat, Trumpeter swung his cold gaze to the Dragoon lieutenant. Although haggard, travel-stained and dishevelled from long exertions, the young officer was not wounded in any way.

"How did you come to escape, mister?"

"I didn't escape—" the lieutenant answered, cheeks reddening at the implications which he read into the question.

"You call me 'sir!'" Trumpeter barked.

"I didn't escape—*sir*," the lieutenant answered, stiffening into a brace. "We were *all* released by the Confederates. They mostly turn their captives loose out there. Captain Fog even—"

"*Who?*"

Trumpeter almost screeched the word as he leapt to his feet. Dropping back a hurried, involuntary stride, the lieutenant threw a startled glance at Verncombe. Then the young officer stared at the general's shocked, white face. A long thirty seconds went by before the lieutenant could think up and make his reply.

"Ca-Captain Dusty Fog, sir. It was him who took us from the rear and captured the battery."

"Are you sure it was him?" Trumpeter asked, struggling to regain his pose of imperturbability. He sank into his chair and waited for the answer, hoping against hope that the lieutenant was wrong.

"There's no doubt of it, sir," the young Dragoon replied. "It was Company "C" of the Texas Light Cavalry; although it came as a helluva—a real surprise when I learned who he was."

"How's that?" Trumpeter spat out.

"I'd always heard he was a giant of a man. But he's small and not more than eighteen at the most. Only when he speaks to you, you forget about him being small. And you should have seen how those Texans jumped when he spoke to them—"

"Yes!" Trumpeter interrupted testily, wondering when last anybody had jumped to obey *his* commands.

All too well the general remembered Savos' and Hoffinger's descriptions of their captor. Each of them had commented at length on Dusty Fog's small size and laid much emphasis on the fact that his personality had caused the captives to forget such minor details as feet and inches of height. It seemed unlikely that there could be three, or even two, Confederate cavalry captains so identical in appearance on the Arkansas battle-front. Much as Trumpeter hated to face the fact, he knew that Captain Dusty Fog had once again been responsible for ruining his plans for aggrandizement.

"They turned us loose, sir," the lieutenant went on, determined to exculpate himself from the unspoken insult Trumpeter had laid on him. "Even gave us horses and made litters to carry our wounded. Captain Fog talked to me while his men and the Arkansas Rifles started to erect defences on the rim above our positions. It was he who mentioned the forged orders, sir. From what he implied, the Rebels knew they were fakes, but acted on them to capture the battery and our side of the ford. As soon as we were out of sight of the Rebels, I took the best of the horses and rode as fast as I could to report to Colonel Verncombe."

"How about it?" Verncombe went on. "Did you have the fake orders passed out, general?"

Overlooking the fact that the colonel spoke in a manner anything but polite or militarily correct when addressing a one-star brigadier general, Trumpeter shook his head. If Fog had spoken the truth, the Rebels must have suspected the man who delivered the forged document. With luck, he had been killed not captured. At any rate, Trumpeter had no intention of admitting his connection with the abortive attempt, especially to a subordinate officer and career soldier.

"I know nothing about it," the general lied. "If the—"

Never had a knock on the door been so welcome to Trumpeter's ears turning from Verncombe's accusing eyes, he called for whoever knocked to come in.

"Lieutenant Silverman of the Zouaves is here, sir,' Trumpeter's aide announced on entering. "He's asked to see you on a matter of extreme urgency."

"Show the lieutenant in, Mr. Frost," Trumpeter ordered, only too pleased to be given a chance to dismiss the Dragoons. "If you gentlemen will excu—"

Before the "gentlemen" could be sent from the room, Silverman entered. Of middle height, he was stocky, sallow-faced and wore an untidy uniform. Like the Dragoon lieutenant, he gave the impression of having done some hard, fast travelling. Being of "liberal" persuasions, he had burst in on Trumpeter, wishing to flaunt his success in the faces of the two Dragoon career soldiers who Frost had told him were present. In his left hand, he held three sheets of paper which Trumpeter thought looked unpleasantly familiar.

"Sir!" Silverman said, coming to a halt, saluting and offering the papers almost in one movement. "While on patrol along the Caddo River, I came into possession of these orders issued by Hardin. He's planning an offensive and has ordered attacks on three fords along the Ouachita."

Fighting to hold down his emotions, Trumpeter had to force himself to take the papers from Silverman's hand. Then he stared at them as if mesmerized. Without any doubt, as he saw straight away, they were the orders forged with such care and attention to detail at his instigation in Washington. Not until certain that he had composed his features into an impassive, blank mask did the general look at the beaming Silverman. From the expression on the Zouave's Hebraic face, he expected praise and commendation for his actions.

"How did you come by these?" Trumpeter asked, hoping that his voice sounded less strained to the listeners than it did to his own ears.

"From a guerilla I met on the Ouachita," Silverman explained. "I was on my way to commence a patrol when I met him. He's a good man who circumstances prevented from enlisting in the Army—"

"What kind of circumstances?" grunted Verncombe.

"I don't think we need concern ourselves with that, Colonel," Trumpeter put in coldly. "Go on, Mr. Silverman!"

"As soon as I saw the contents of the orders—" Silverman began.

"You came rushing here with them," Verncombe finished for him. "Didn't you think that you should warn the men guarding the fords?"

"I—I sent my sergeant to do that," Silverman answered sullenly. "And, anyway, as I had the orders it didn't seem likely that the attacks would be made. So I came here as fast as I could to hand them over to General Trumpeter."

"You did the right thing, Mr. Silverman," Trumpeter praised, although he wished that the other had come at a more opportune moment or waited until the Dragoons had left the office before displaying his trophies. "I'll mark your report to that effect."

Despite his general's approval, Silverman could see that Colonel Verncombe was less impressed with his brilliant grasp of the situation and prompt action. The Dragoon eyed him coldly and said:

"Mister, I hope for your sake that your sergeant reached the fords in time to give a warning—or that those orders are fakes."

"Fa—Fakes?" Silverman yelped, thinking of the fifty dollars he had paid for them. "Good man" or not, the guerilla had insisted on being remunerated for his trouble before handing them over.

"It's a possibility, Mr. Silverman," Trumpeter admitted. "They may have been put out by our Secret Service—"

"Which means that your guerilla friend killed one of our spies, mister," Verncombe went on.

"Mr. Silverman couldn't know that, Colonel!" Trumpeter interrupted coldly. "He acted correctly and in a manner which I approve. We don't know that these are fakes.

After all, whoever was killed must have delivered the first set of orders and been allowed to go on with the others."

"Not necessarily—sir," Verncombe objected. "How loyal is that guerilla of yours, mister?"

"I—I've never dealt with him before," Silverman answered warily. "But I've heard good reports about him from other officers. He told me that he'd killed the Rebel courier on the other side of the river and I'd no cause to think he lied."

"Of course, he wouldn't offer you anything that might show the orders were forged, would he?" Verncombe demanded.

"I—I don't follow you, sir," Silverman muttered.

"If he'd killed a courier on his way to Ole Devil with the forged orders and a report, he'd know they wouldn't be worth anything to him," Verncombe explained. "So he wouldn't say anything about it."

"It's possible," Trumpeter admitted, willing to clutch at any straw as long as it held the conversation away from his share in the responsibility. "Did he say or do anything to make you think he might have other documents taken from the courier?"

"No—sir," Silverman answered, applying the honorific as Trumpeter showed disapproval of its omission by *him* for the first time. "If he'd had any more, I'm sure he'd have passed them on."

"Unless he figured he could get a better price somewhere else," Verncombe sniffed, for he had no illusions about the loyalty or honesty of the average guerilla leader.

"As I said, Colonel," Trumpeter declared when Verncombe swung to face him. "I know nothing about forged orders. Perhaps the plan to use them was made in General Buller's time?"

"*You* ordered the artillery to move up," Verncombe pointed out.

"Yes," admitted Trumpeter, thinking faster than ever before in his life. "I found an order left by General Buller for reinforcing the four fords with batteries of artillery and put it through. It was possible that there were developments afoot of which I hadn't been informed."

Opening his mouth to ask another question, Verncombe closed it with the words unsaid. Already he had gone to the very boundaries of military etiquette and a demand that he be shown Buller's order might lead to his facing a court-martial for gross insubordination. From his wary attitude, Trumpeter had recovered after the first shock at seeing the documents. He could be counted on to know how he might best defend himself against criticism—no matter how justified—by an officer of lower rank.

"You wanted to say something, Colonel?" Trumpeter challenged.

"Only to ask for orders, sir," Verncombe replied blandly, figuring that if the commanding general could lie he was at liberty to do so. "Mr. Aston says that the Rebels were making preparations to hold the eastern bank of the Snake Ford. What action does the general plan to take—sir?"

Ignoring the thinly-veiled sarcasm in his subordinate's voice, Trumpeter quickly marshalled the facts and tried to reach a decision. The Snake Ford of the Caddo had little military significance. Two of the reasons for selecting that area had been its lack of importance and distance from the main battle-zone. So, on the face of it, there seemed little need and no urgency to act. For all that, he knew there could be only one answer. As long as the Rebels occupied the eastern side of the ford, they would be a constant reminder of his failure. Not knowing of his thwarted grand plan, people would only remember that his predecessors had at least managed to hold on to the land already captured.

So, regardless of the cost to his command, the Rebels must be driven back to the western bank. Looking at Verncombe's cold, impassive face, Trumpeter saw a chance of taking his revenge on the colonel.

"Your regiment will retake the ford, Colonel Verncombe," Trumpeter announced with the air of one conferring a favour.

"We'll need artillery support—sir," Verncombe answered, aware of the general's intentions and the price for failure.

"There are three batteries at the neighbouring fords," Trumpeter told him. "I'll give you an order for them. Then you'll have all the support you need."

CHAPTER NINE

They've Captured Mrs. Greenhow

General Jackson Baines Hardin, better known as Old Devil, was a tall, slim, tanned man who sat the chair behind his desk as if riding in full review. Hawk-faced, with eyes that hinted at a sense of humour under the grim mask, he was a different kind of soldier to his opposite number across the Ouachita. Tough, hard as nails, strict without being a blind martinet, Ole Devil Hardin had won the respect of his men on the battle-field and by his interest in their welfare.

Nothing on his face showed his feelings, or that he was studying his favourite nephew carefully, but he nodded in satisfaction as Captain Dusty Fog completed a verbal report on the recent activities of Company "C."

It was over a week since the capture of the Snake Ford from the Yankees and during that time Dusty's Company had taken a major part in defending the rim above the river. Ole Devil had been in full agreement with the decision to hold the recovered territory and had acted with characteristic speed. Reinforcements, including trained artillerymen to take over the Napoleons, had been rushed to the Caddo. Their arrival increased the already serious problems faced by Colonel Verncombe. Already the Dragoons had been delayed by lack of artillery support. On their return from delivering the warnings about the forged orders, Red Blaze and Kiowa had crossed the Ouachita and succeeded in running off every horse belonging to the batteries brought up to repulse the attacks which never came. By doing so, they had deprived Verncombe of the cannons at a time when they would have done him most good.

After an unsupported attack at regimental strength had failed, due to the fire from the captured Napoleons, Verncombe had found his men disinclined to take further risks. Just as Dusty had hoped, the story he had started circulated amongst the Dragoons. It caused much discontent, especially from the long-serving career-soldiers, and considerable cursing over the "college-boy" general's stupidity in trying such an impractical, easily detected trick. The Dragoons were grudging of their lives and unwilling to face death to recapture land that ought never to have fallen to the enemy in the first place.

"By the time they'd got artillery with them, sir, so had we and trained gun crews to man the first battery," Dusty concluded, then went on after a brief pause, "Colonel Barnett's handled things real well all the way through, sir."

"Has he?" Old Devil grunted coldly.

"Yes, sir. I know he had both of his mounted couriers away at the same time, but he's infantry. Horses don't mean a thing to him."

"He was fooled by those forged orders—"

"Anybody would've been, sir. You've seen them and know how good they are. The signature on them is so near perfect that *I* couldn't see any difference between it and the real thing."

"That wasn't what you told Barnett," Old Devil pointed out.

"No, sir," Dusty admitted. "Only I had to say something that would convince him it was a forgery. So I took a chance on him figuring, me being your nephew, that I'd be able to tell. It paid off— And that he obeyed in spite of the cavalry not reporting to him's a mighty high tribute to *you*, sir."

Giving a non-committal grunt, Ole Devil looked at the papers on his desk so that Dusty might not see any hint of the pride he felt at his nephew's behaviour. Many young officers would have been determined to grab the fullest amount of glory for themselves from the incident at the Snake Ford, but Dusty's primary interest was to help Barnett out of his difficulties.

"I think we can forget the matter," the general said

gruffly. "Whatever happens to Colonel Barnett, if anything, is none of your concern, Captain Fog."

"No, sir," Dusty replied.

Yet Ole Devil's words had told him that Barnett's career
would not suffer as a result of being taken in by the forged
order. Having cleared up that point, Dusty wondered why
his Company had been replaced at the ford and he had
received orders to report as quickly as possible to General
Hardin's headquarters at Prescott. With his report finished,
he did not expect to be kept waiting long before he learned
the reason.

"You've heard of Mrs. Rose Greenhow, Dustine?" Ole
Devil asked.

"She's one of our best spies, isn't she, sir?"

"She is," Old Devil agreed. Less hide-bound than most
Confederate senior officers, he admitted that women spies
served a useful purpose; although he did not entirely approve of Southern ladies performing such unpleasant and
dangerous work. "She's coming to report to me with information about Trumpeter and other matters. So I want her
collected from Wexler's place—"

"Is she in Little Rock already, sir?"

"She will be by the time you get there, according to my
information. She's coming by stagecoach, traveling as a
Yankee major's wife on her way to join him. Naturally she
doesn't want to stay in Little Rock any longer than necessary. So I want you to travel fast, meet her and bring her
here."

"Yes, sir. It shouldn't be too hard. The Yankees've
taken most of their troops along the Ouachita up to the
Snake Ford, so getting across'll be easy enough. I'll not
take the full Company. A small party can travel faster. Do
you reckon Mrs. Greenhow can ride?"

"She can, if what I've heard of her is true," Old Devil
confirmed. "But I doubt if she'll be up to your Cousin
Betty's standard."

"That's not likely, sir," Dusty grinned.

"No, it's not," the general admitted, for his grand-
daughter possessed exceptional ability as a horsewoman.

"Pick her horses carefully and don't expect too much and you should get her through. By the way, Dustine, Betty and Georgina Blaze are expected to arrive any day now on a visit."

"Let's hope they don't get here until after Mrs. Greenhow's gone, sir," Dusty drawled. "If they do, she's likely to wind up with another couple of lady spies."

"Not if I've anything to say about it," Ole Devil stated, smiling frostily. Like Dusty, he knew the two girls to be high-spirited and likely to snatch at the opportunity to take a more active part in the war against the Yankees. Then he became serious again. "I don't need to tell you how important it is that Mrs. Greenhow is kept out of the Union's clutches, Dustine."

"No, sir. Now, with your permission, I'll go and pick the men I want with me. We'll be on our way before sundown."

"Thanks for the bay stallion, Dustine," Ole Devil remarked as the small Texan saluted and turned to leave the office. "Only you didn't need to send word that it has to be saddled and mounted from the right. *I* know all Indian horses do."

"I figured you might, sir," Dusty answered with a grin.

"And you'd better take half of your ill-gotten gambling gains with you," Old Devil concluded, also smiling. "Wexler can probably find use for it."

Leaving Ole Devil and making his way to Company "C"'s lines, Dusty pondered on the vagaries of a cavalry officer's life. There had been much speculation amongst his men on the subject of their recall. The reasons suggested had ranged from the optimistic, that they were to be sent back to Texas on furlough, through the dramatic, that they would be spear-heading an offensive aimed at driving the Yankees clear back to Washington, to Billy Jack's pessimistic view that they were all to be court-martialled for fraternizing and gambling with the enemy. When Dusty had been asked to guess what quirk of fate took them back to Headquarters, the idea that it was to collect a female spy from the heart of Union territory had never entered his head. Yet, as Ole Devil had warned, the mission was of considerable importance.

Along with Belle Boyd—in whose company Dusty would later go on two dangerous missions*—Rose Greenhow ranked high in the Confederate States' Secret Service. Between them, originally in the face of official antipathy and disapproval, they had built up an organization which had caused the Union Army a great deal of trouble. Despite the objections of various senior officers and members of the Government, the two Southern ladies had more than justified the wisdom of employing them as spies. The Yankees would be most pleased to lay hands on either Belle Boyd† or Rose Greenhow if the chance arose, for both of them possessed information that could all but wipe out the Confederate's Secret Service.

For all that, Dusty felt little concern over his assignment. Without falling into the trap of over-confidence, he felt certain that he could once again cross the Ouachita, pass undetected through the Union-held country, reach Little Rock and return. The way he saw it, as long as Rose Greenhow could handle a horse at least adequately, bringing her to Prescott would present him with no serious problems or difficulties.

Ordering a protesting, but obedient, Red Blaze and Billy Jack to take charge of the Company, Dusty selected his escort. Kiowa Cotton, Corporals Vern Hassle and Sandy McGraw expressed their delight on finding that they would be accompanying Dusty instead of remaining in the safety of the regiment's camp at Prescott. Stifling Red's and other members of the Company's reasons for inclusion in the party, Dusty kept his destination to himself. He made his arrangements with the speed born of experience.

The journey to the rendezvous passed without incident or alarm. Each of the party rode a two-horse relay and the corporals also led a mount apiece to be used by Rose

---

*Told in *The Colt and the Sabre* and *The Rebel Spy*.

†More of Belle's history is told in *The Bloody Border* and *The Bad Bunch*.

Greenhow on the return trip. Wanting to make the best possible speed, they carried only the bare essentials. Sabres and carbines had been left behind, although Dusty had brought along his Henry rifle. Their bedding was restricted to a single blanket and poncho, with a spare taken for Rose's use. For food they would rely on pemmican,* the nourishing "Indian-bread" which could be easily carried, and anything that came their way. Dusty had with him two more items, a Union Army cloak-coat and officer's fatigue cap, but they were for a practical purpose rather than added luxuries for his comfort.

Travelling fast, for their mounts were the pick of the Texas Light Cavalry's extensive remuda, they had seen no Union troops. At night-fall on the day after leaving their headquarters, Dusty left the corporals and horses hidden in the wooded country half a mile to the east of Little Rock. Dressed in the cloak-coat and fatigue cap, the former hiding his uniform and armament, Dusty went forward on foot. Devoid of any disguise, Kiowa drifted along like a shadow on Dusty's heels; ready to fade into the darkness should they meet anybody.

Approaching a wooden building on the outskirts of the town, Dusty became even more cautious. While a lantern hung by the back door, its light turned down to a feeble glimmer, he took no chances. Not until Kiowa had scouted the area and announced all was clear did he go closer. Satisfied that nobody was spying upon him, Dusty crossed to the door and knocked.

"Who's there?" called a querulous voice.

"Lieutenant Oakland, 3rd Cavalry," Dusty replied.

A lock clicked and the door inched open as a thin, sharp, mean-featured face peered out at Dusty.

"Come in, lieutenant," said the owner of the face, opening the door. "A man in my position has to watch who he lets in at night. Those Rebel scum've threatened to kill me."

Grinning slightly at the greeting, Dusty stepped into the work-room of an undertaker's shop. For all his comments,

*One recipe for making pemmican is given in *Commanche*.

Hugo Wexler was the head of the Confederate States' Secret Service in Arkansas.

Small, slender, dressed in sober black, Wexler looked the part of a successful undertaker. In many ways his appearance and occupation helped his work as a spy, but he had another, more valuable asset. Back in the early days of the abolition issue, he had decided that a physical clash between the North and the South could not be avoided. Firmly believing that each State should have the right to secede from the Union if its policies proved incompatible with those of the Federal Government—the major issue of the War, although the abolitionists recognized and used the propaganda value of freeing the slaves as their excuse for entering into hostilities—Wexler had sought for a way to serve the South. Becoming a member of the Radical Republican faction in Arkansas, he had succeeded in convincing them of his complete devotion to their cause.

Facing the derision and hostility of his own people had not been easy, but Wexler held on. At the outbreak of the War, he had "fled" to safety with the other Radicals and returned to resume his business in Little Rock on the heels of the victorious Yankee Army. Everything about his background made him ideally suited to gather valuable information for the South. It had been due to his efforts that Ole Devil Hardin had known the Union Army's weaknesses; a knowledge which allowed him to halt the Yankees' advance on assuming command in Arkansas.

"You should ask for a guard from the Army, Mr. Wexler," Dusty remarked in a loud voice.

"We're alone, Captain," Wexler answered, pleased with the way his visitor remembered to take precautions. "And I've bad news for you. They've captured Mrs. Greenhow."

"The hell you say!" Dusty spat out. "How did it happen?"

"You remember the dude who you took the remounts from?" Wexler asked.

'Sure."

"He was at the stagecoach depot, waiting to leave on the stage that brought Mrs. Greenhow in. As you can imagine, he's not been over-popular with Trumpeter since his failure. Well, it seems that he'd known her in Washington. She's a striking woman, very beautiful and not easily forgotten. Anyway, he recognized her and saw his chance to regain Trumpeter's favour. Before I could contact her, he had fetched the Provost Marshal and denounced her."

"Damn his ornery lil hide," Dusty said quietly. "I near on took him along with us, but I didn't reckon he could've swum a horse across the narrows between the lakes. What happened?"

"I must say Mrs. Greenhow was good," Wexler replied. "She looked shocked and angry, demanded to see the commanding general and for her husband to be informed. It didn't do any good, they took her with them."

"Where're they holding her?"

"In one of the basement cells at the town's jail. It's mainly used for a military prison now."

"What force does Trumpeter have guarding her?"

"Just the normal jail guard and a woman brought in to act as matr—" Wexler began, then he stared at the *big* young Texan who was one of the few people who knew of his secret second identity. "You can't be thinking of attempting a rescue, Captain Fog!"

"I was sent to collect her," Dusty answered. "If there's any way it can be done, I aim to make a try." He paused, then went on, "How's her being captured hit you and your boys, Mr. Wexler?"

"She knows we are in Arkansas, but not much more than that," Wexler replied. "She doesn't know any of our names."

"She's still got to be set free if it can be done," Dusty stated.

"Damn it, I know that!" Wexler snapped. "It's *you* I'm thinking about."

"How do you mean?"

"Mean—Lordy lord! Haven't you heard—?"

"About what?"

"How Trumpeter feels about you after the way you've been cutting up since his arrival in Arkansas."

"Billy Jack did warn me that I'd go riling him," Dusty admitted with a grin.

"*Riling* him!" Wexler croaked, raising his eyes to the roof and shaking his head. "You steal two mortars and shell his grand review, scattering it to hell and gone and make him a laughingstock in front of the civilian population. Then you capture his remounts and he can't get money to buy any more. If that's not enough, you spoil his plan to discredit Ole Devil, causing him to look an imcompetent fool to his men; who don't believe it when he says that he knows nothing about the forged orders. And then you run off the horses from the three batteries of artillery he was relying on to push you back across the Caddo before Ole Devil could reinforce you—"

"That last was Cousin Red, not me," Dusty objected cheerfully.

"This's serious, Captain Fog!" Wexler snapped. "More serious than you know. Trumpeter has sent out an order to all his commanding officers. It made a stir amongst them and they say it's without precedent. I've seen a copy of it and it says, 'No matter how it is done, capture or KILL Dusty Fog!' Captain, the word 'kill' is in capital letters."

"Yes, sir!" Dusty drawled. "Don't you ever tell him, but ole Billy Jack was right. I *have* riled Trumpeter up."

"Damn it, Captain!" the agent yelped. "He means every word of that order—and with most of his officers, it will be 'kill,' not 'capture'!"

A half smile played on Dusty's lips and he seemed unconcerned by the threat to his life. Not that he discounted its danger. There were many Union officers in Arkansas with reason to hate him and who would be willing to carry out their general's order given half a chance.

"I'll just have to go extra careful," Dusty remarked. "But I'm going for all of that."

"I've told you the dangers," Wexler said simply.

"Why sure," Dusty agreed. "Which I'm not fixing to charge the jail-house at the head of Company "C," sabres drawn and flags flying. But we both know that we've got to get Mrs. Greenhow out if we can."

"That goes without saying."

"Then let's figure out how we can do it. How's she guarded?"

"With just the normal jail-house staff right now. A sergeant and six corporals—"

"No more than that?" Dusty breathed.

"They're trained men, from Army stockades."

"Which means they'll be tough, mean, but not too smart," Dusty commented. "As long as that's all the guard on her."

"It is, although they brought the wife of a sergeant to act as matron," Wexler answered. "Trumpeter has stripped the town's garrison to give strength to a massive assault on the Snake Ford, he's even emptied the cells of prisoners for it. Don't look so worried, I've already sent warning to Colonel Barnett that it's coming."

"Just seven men," Dusty said quietly. "And a woman, maybe. I'd've expected more than that."

"In addition to being short of men in the town garrison right now, Trumpeter believes that Mrs. Greenhow's capture is a secret," Wexler explained. "Probably he also assumes that, even if we found out, we'd never expect him to put a Southern lady into a common jail-house. So he doesn't want to attract attention by increasing the guard."

"That figures," Dusty admitted. "Tell me all you know about the jail; how it's guarded, the routine the guards follow, when they get fed and how, everything that might help. Maybe we can think up some way to get her loose."

"I hope we can," Wexler said sincerely.

"There's another thing we've got to think about," Dusty warned. "Trumpeter won't like it one lil bit if we bring it off. He'll want blood and it'll be the Lord help you happen he found out who you are."

"That's a chance I have to take," Wexler answered. "Risking being found out is something I've come to live with."

While Dusty accepted that, he knew a successful rescue would rouse Trumpeter to such a pitch of fury that the Yankees were going to hunt as never before for the people responsible. While Rose Greenhow's freedom might be of considerable importance to the South, so was Wexler's. Somehow, Dusty could not think how right then, he must find a way to divert suspicion from the little undertaker if the rescue bid should be brought off.

Suddenly a thought came to Dusty, driving the concern he felt for Wexler's safety momentarily from his mind.

"Say, not long back I read something in a Yankee newspaper about stockade guards being in trouble with the softshells."

A frown creased the undertaker's brow. He did not answer for some seconds, then he realized what Dusty meant.

"That's true, they were and still are," Wexler finally agreed. "I didn't bother to report it to General Hardin, it didn't seem important enough."

"I don't know about that," Dusty drawled. "It may just be important enough to help us prise Mrs. Greenhow loose from that old jail-house."

CHAPTER TEN

He Needs Teaching Respect For His Betters

Disregarding the scowls of the other enlisted men present, Sergeant Bernie Slasser and Corporal Dick Pope swaggered into the Birdcage Cafe for their supper. Although the owner secretly wished that they would go elsewhere, he stood by their usual table and greeted them politely. Big, burly, with brutish faces and close-cropped hair, they wore Burnside hats and infantry uniforms; but every soldier in the room knew to which branch of the Army they belonged. Stockade guards had never been selected for charm of personality and understanding natures. Alertness and caution had become a way of life with the pair. Their hands never strayed far from the twenty-six inch long oak batons dangling from loops and balancing the holstered revolvers on their belts. Aware that every man in the room most likely hated their guts, the knowledge caused Slasser and Pope no concern.

"It's a nice night, gentlemen," greeted the owner, grinning with patent insincerity.

"You're getting your share of it," Slasser grunted, hanging his hat on the back of a chair and sitting down. "We'll want a meal to take back. Nothing fancy and don't hurry it. If it's not ready, the fellers we relieve can fetch it."

"I understand, sergeant," the owenr replied truthfully. "Do you gentlemen want your usual?"

"It's no worse than any of the other hawg-wash you serve," Pope growled and, after the man had left, grinned at his companion. "Did you see that Southern gal?"

"Not enough," Slasser answered. "We can go take a look later. Sarah'll've gone then."

100

"It'd be best if we waited until we knew what the Man*
has to say about her first," Pope suggested cautiously.
"He's wetting his pants on the hour about correct procedure
since the top brass sent out that damned order about how
we treat the prisoners."

"There's only one way to treat a prisoner," Slasser spat
out. "Rough."

Pope darted a quick glance around, as if wishing to
make sure that nobody had heard his companion's comment. Then he let the subject lapse and the arrival of their
food prevented Slasser from resuming it. While eating,
their alertness never left them. Continually flickering their
eyes around the room, they gave the impression that they
were studying the soldiers to select the ones most likely to
fall into their hands. Neither of them showed any great
interest when, at the conclusion of their meal, a seedy-
looking civilian sidled over to their table. Poorly-dressed,
prone to giving a hacking cough at regular intervals, he
was assistant to one of the sutlers who followed and traded
with the soldiers.

"Sergeant—" the man began, bobbing his head ingra-
tiatingly after a preliminary cough.

"What's up, Hacker?" Slasser demanded.

"Air that bounty on deserters still getting paid?"

"Sure," the sergeant agreed, interest replacing his
frown. The Union Army offered a reward of a hundred
dollars to anybody who was responsible for the capture of a
deserter. "Why?"

"Nothing," Hacker replied, starting to turn away. "I was
just ask—"

Shooting out a big hand, Slasser caught the civilian's
thin arm and crushed it. "Where is he, Hacker?"

"I—I—" the man answered, then he gave a resigned
shrug. "He's in here."

"Which one?" Pope inquired.

"See that short runt sat near the front door?" Hacker
answered, without looking at or indicating the person he

---

*The Man: in this case, the Provost Marshal.

meant. "He's the one. Used to be with Custer's outfit. Owed my boss money, which's how I 'member him.''

Without displaying too obvious interest, the two stockade guards turned and studied the man in question. Small, though well-built, young, with a bare head of curly blond hair, he wore a collarless shirt and poorly-fitting cheap civilian suit. For the most part, he looked like an ordinary youngster from the working-class section of the town. Only one thing pointed to Hacker's statement being correct. His boots, which showed from under the table, were of better quality than the rest of his wardrobe indicated. There was another sign which the experienced pair could recognize. While waiting for his food to arrive, the youngster kept his head bent forward except when darting flickering, furtive glances around the room.

"Why'd a deserter come here to eat?" Pope asked.

"Likely he thinks this's the last place anybody'd expect to find a feller who's gone over the hill," Hacker offered.

"Them's cavalry boots he's wearing, Popey," Slasser went on. "Even if he ain't a deserter, it'd be interesting learning where he got 'em. Let's go over and see what he's got to say for his-self."

"You won't forget it was me's pointed him out, will-ya?" whined Hacker as the non-coms came to their feet and put their hats on.

"We'll not forget," Slasser promised, winking at his companion. "If he's a deserter, we'll see the right thing's done."

Seated at the table with his back to the wall, Dusty Fog watched the by-play between the civilian and the two soldiers. Nothing about him showed that he was aware of their scrutiny and interest. As a waiter placed a steaming plate of stew before him, he grinned and tensed. The first stage of Mrs. Greenhow's rescue had begun.

As always, Wexler had proved to possess plenty of vitally important information about the current situation. Admitting that he had expected Dusty to attempt a rescue bid—and ready to try himself if the other had not arrived that night—the undertaker had already gathered in details of the woman's incarceration. He had previously collected a thorough working knowledge of the jail's routine in case it might one day be needed. Working from what he had been able to tell Dusty, a daring scheme was concocted. There had been little enough time to arrange its details, but so far everything was going correctly.

Surreptitiously watching the soldiers drawing closer, with Hacker following on their heels, Dusty measured the distance between them with his eyes. Give them their due, they were putting on a mighty good act. Neither showed any obvious interest in him and they were acting in a casual manner as if merely leaving the cafe. An unsuspecting victim might have been fooled by them. Aware of what was going on, Dusty made ready to play his part. None of the other occupants of the room were watching the stockade guards right then, but Dusty figured that he ought to be able to draw attention their way.

In a casual-appearing gesture, Dusty rested the palms of his hands under the edge of the table. Then he glanced up and down and jerked back his head in a startled manner, as if suddenly becoming aware of the two non-coms bearing down on him. Catching his cue with the skill of a professional actor, Hacker went on with the next part of the scheme. In addition to being a sutler's assistant, he was one of Wexler's most trusted agents.

"That's him for certain sure, sergeant!" Hacker yelled. "He's over the hill from Custer's outfit!"

Letting out an annoyed grunt, Slasser lunged forward. He had hoped to be within reaching distance before the "deserter" realized the danger, but Hacker's shouted comment ruined his chances of doing it. So he advanced, meaning to reach over the table and grab the small young man. Despite being alerted, he could hardly escape. The wall prevented him from backing away.

Not that Dusty meant to try escaping in that manner. Instead he heaved upwards with his hands, throwing the table over. His aim could hardly have been better if he had practised the move for days. Shooting off the inclined surface, the plate of stew distributed its hot contents over the

front of Slasser's tunic. Nor did the damage end there. In
falling, the edge of the table cracked against the shin-bone
of the sergeant's forward leg. Going by the screech Slasser
let out, the impact caused him considerable pain.

Having dealt with Slasser in a most satisfactory manner
Dusty came to his feet. For his plan to succeed, he had to
make what seemed a determined attempt to escape, but
without antagonizing Corporal Pope. So he contented himself with evading the other's hands and resisted the temptation to deliver a *karate* attack. Ducking by Pope, Dusty ran
towards the door. Bounding forward, Hacker thrust out his
right leg to trip and bring the small Texan sprawling to the
floor.

"Fix the bastard good, Pope!" Slasser bellowed, hop-
ping on his sound leg and massaging the injured shin.
"Tromp him into the ground!"

Elbowing Hacker aside, Pope held down an inclination
to carry out his sergeant's instructions. All around the
room, feet shuffled, chairs scraped and men stood up hurriedly to obtain a better view of what was happening. Re-
fraining from driving his boot into Dusty's body, Pope bent
to grip the collar of his borrowed jacket and jerked him
erect. Seeing the burly guard raise the small youngster and
slam him against the wall, an angry, menacing growl rose
from the on-lookers. Only a few of the closest soldiers
knew what had started the fuss, but their attitude mirrored
that of the remainder. Maybe they had little sympathy with
deserters, but they actively hated and despised the stockade
guards.

Knowing how the enlisted men felt, Pope decided to do
no more than haul his captive upright. Pope might be as
hard, tough and unimaginative a roughneck as ever
guarded military prisoners, but he possessed sufficient
sense to see the danger. If he should start to work the small
"deserter" over with feet or fists, the crowd would intervene. There were men present only seeking the opportunity
to tangle with members of the stockade guard, yet they
formed the least serious threat to his way of thinking.
Others would be just as eager to witness an incident that

could be reported to those "liberal" Congressmen who took an interest in and gave protection to the "under-dog." Under the prevailing conditions, Pope had no desire to antagonize the latter group of his audience.

Mouthing obscenities, Slasser prepared to fly in the face of popular opinion. Hot stew soaked and clung to his tunic, while pain throbbed through his shin. Added to that was the knowledge that almost every man in the room revelled at the sight of his injury and humiliation. It all served to rouse his never too amiable temper to a furious pitch.

For the first time, Dusty wondered if the plan was going wrong. Seeing the big sergeant looming at him, he hoped that nothing had happened to keep Wexler from carrying out the part assigned to him. Crouching against the wall with an attitude of numb terror, Dusty prepared to launch a devastating *karate* attack to protect himself. To do so would ruin the rescue bid and endanger his own safety.

Even as Dusty tensed to drive up his foot, he saw the front door open. So did Slasser, and recognized the two men who entered. With a feeling of baffled frustration, the sergeant scowled at the newcomers and revised his intention of teaching the "deserter" an immediate and painful lesson. Neither Trumpeter's aide, 1st Lieutenant Frost, nor that mealy-mouthed soft-shell undertaker would stand by and watch while he battered the small son-of-a-bitch to a pulp.

If Frost had been alone, he would have ignored the disturbance he heard while passing the Birdcage Cafe. The place was a hangout for enlisted men and going in without an escort to quell the trouble could be dangerous. Unfortunately he had just met Wexler and the undertaker insisted that they should investigate. Knowing that Wexler possessed some influence, even in military circles, Frost dare not refuse. Reluctantly, he opened the door and stepped inside.

When Frost saw the men responsible for the noise, he realized the advantages of intervening. Firstly, another soft-shell stood at his side. Knowing how he would act in similar circumstances, he believed that Wexler would enjoy making an adverse report to General Trumpeter if he failed to protect the small victim. Secondly, he had the typical liberal-intellectual's hatred of those whom he regarded as the tools and implements of authority. While willing to make use of the stockade guards for his own ends, he despised them at other times. Third and most important, to prevent Slasser from attacking the terrified youngster would raise Frost in the esteem of the watching enlisted men. One never knew, during some future election men in the crowd might remember the incident and be persuaded to vote for him.

So Frost fixed Slasser with a cold glare, wanting to remind the other that a lieutenant was backed by the disciplinary powers of *The Manual Of Field Regulations,* and barked, "What's all this?"

"We've been told this bastard's a deserter," Slasser answered, coming to a surly, grudging brace. "Was going to ask him about it when he jumped us and tried to escape."

"Did good at it, too!" called a voice from the crowd.

"Are you a deserter?" Frost asked Dusty as Slasser swung around furiously in an attempt to recognize the speaker.

Knowing that the small Texan's voice might spoil the deception. Hacker was prepared to give confirmation. The need did not arise. Wanting to prove that they had not acted hastily, Pope stepped forward and threw up a smarter-than-usual salute.

"Sure he is, lieutenant, sir," the corporal declared and pointed to the floor. "Look at them boots. They're U.S. cavalry issue."

A point with which Dusty could not have truly argued, considering they had been looted from a Yankee convoy. While he had borrowed the civilian clothing from a store of such things kept by Wexler, he had retained the boots as offering proof of Hacker's accusation.

"They're cavalry boots, no doubt about that," Frost admitted. "Who told you that he's a deserter?"

"Hacker there," Slasser muttered.

"Now that ain't entirely right, sergeant," the gaunt man

objected, then faced Frost and bobbed his head in a respectful manner the officer found most gratifying. "I only said he *looked* like a feller I knowed in the 7th Cavalry, sir. My boss'd know for certain sure, but he's out of town for a couple of days."

Dusty made a feeble escape to free himself from Pope's hand, taking care not to be too violent or to hurt the other, and quitting when he was banged back against the wall. Looking what he hoped was sullenly and guiltily at Frost, Dusty tried to will the other into reaching the correct decision.

"Have you ever seen this youngster around Little Rock, Mr. Wexler?" Frost inquired.

"Well, I can't be sure," Wexler dithered. "But I don't recall ever seeing him. And, even if he is a local boy, where did he get those boots from?"

"There's that," Frost admitted and looked at Dusty. "What have you to say?"

"Nothing!" Dusty mumbled, trying to avoid sounding like a Texan. "Lemme go."

"Not without a better account of yourself than that!" Frost snapped. "Take him to the cells and hold him, sergeant. We'll see how a night there loosens his tongue."

"Yes, sir!" Slasser replied, with more enthusiasm than he had shown since Frost entered the cafe.

Catching hold of Dusty's right arm, Slasser held it firmly while Pope fanned his hands over his person in search of weapons. Finding none, he gripped Dusty by the other arm. Holding him between them, the guards led him to the door.

"I hope that nothing will happen to the young man, Mr. Frost," Wexler remarked in a carrying voice. "There are so many stories about how prisoners are treated in the stockades."

"Not in our stockade!" Frost protested. "He won't be harmed as long as he behaves himself."

Letting out a low grunt that might have meant anything, Slasser opened the door and they hustled Dusty through it. On the sidewalk, the sergeant slipped his baton free and hefted it almost lovingly. His leg still stung sufficiently to act as a reminder of his grievance. Baring his teeth in a mirthless grimace, he glared viciously at Dusty.

"All right, you short-growed son-of-a-bitch," the sergeant snarled. "Now I'm going to beat the—"

More cautious than his companions, Pope kept his eyes on the building they had just quit. And he had expected, he saw Frost and Wexler watching them through a window. While he did not particularly care what happened to Slasser, he figured that he might be held jointly responsible should the other make an unprovoked attack upon their prisoner.

"Not here, damn it!" Pope warned. "They're watching you. That stinking son-of-a-bitch Frost'd break us both if you laid a hand on him."

"Yeah," rumbled Slasser, returning the baton to its sling. "Only what happens when there's no witnesses's another thing. He needs teaching respect for his betters, Popey, don't he?"

"Could be," Pope grunted, without his usual enthusiasm for such a pleasant pastime. "Let's get him down there. The boys're waiting to be relieved."

In the cafe, Wexler watched the men lead Dusty off along the street. So far everything had gone according to plan, although he wondered what Dusty had thought about the delay in his arrival. It had been all for the best. Seeing Frost coming in his direction, Wexler had waited for him. While Slasser might have held off his attack in the presence of an influential local "soft-shell," he was more likely to refrain if he saw an officer. There was something further for Wexler to do before he had finished with Frost.

"Would you care for a meal, Mr. Frost?'" the undertaker offered. "I was going to the Grand Hotel for supper, why not join me?"

"That's good of you, Mr. Wexler," Frost replied. "I don't mind if I do."

Unnoticed by Slasser or Pope, although expected by Dusty, Hacker came from an alley alongside the cafe. For once the thin man did not cough, but moved in silence as he followed the guards and their "prisoner." Keeping his distance and acting in a normal manner, Hacker tailed them to the main square on the far side of which the jail-house was situated. Up to there Hacker had found no difficulty in trailing along behind the trio. Only a few people used the square and they were all on the opposite side. So he continued with extra care and remained undetected. From what he could see, there would be no chance of following beyond the building next to the jail. It was the City Bank and a lamp inside its farther window threw light across the sidewalk. Not wishing to pass through the illuminated area, Hacker came to a halt and stepped into the mouth of the bank's side alley. From his position, he could see the big building which served as a court as well as housing prisoners. Most of it lay in darkness, unoccupied for the night, but a lamp hung over the side door and a light showed at one of the windows towards the rear.

Standing like a statue in the darkness, Hacker watched the sergeant and corporal escort Dusty to the side door. It opened at Slasser's knock and they hustled the small Texan inside. When the door closed, Hacker sucked in a deep breath. Captain Fog had got that far. The most dangerous part of the rescue bid lay ahead.

Never had time gone so slowly for Hacker. At last the door opened and men came out. Although not five minutes had elapsed since Dusty's disappearance into the jail-house, it seemed far longer to the gaunt man. Counting the uniformed figures as they emerged, Hacker took a heavy leather purse from his jacket's pocket. Tossing it into the air and catching it, so that it gave off a faint jingling, he looked around to make sure that he was unobserved.

"What a way to treat good money!" he mused and skidded the purse along the sidewalk until it halted on the edge of the lighted area. "They can't miss seeing it there. I should pitch horseshoes that good."

With that he withdrew deeper into the alley. Flattening himself against the bank's wall, he listened to the heavy feet thudding on the sidewalk. The sound drew closer and Hacker could hear men talking as they walked. Knowing they were the guards relieved by Slasser and Pope, he strained his ears to catch their conversation.

"To hell with helping Slasser work that runt over," were the first audible words to reach the listener. "Not after what the Man told us."

"He's set on doing it regardless," another of the party went on. "Well, that's up to him and Pope."

"Popey won't help him," declared a third. "And if Slasser does it—"

"You can bet he will, after what that runt did to him," stated the first speaker. "Whooee! I'd've loved to see it."

"If he does it, somebody else'll be wearing the sergeant's bars comes noon tomorrow," continued the third guard, in a tone which implied that he expected to be the "somebody." "Slasser's riled enough to— Hey, what's this on the sidewalk?"

"It's a purse," announced the first speaker as the feet came to a halt. "A good heavy one at that."

"Feller it belongs to must've dropped it when he come out of the bank," guessed a fourth voice. "What'll we do with it?"

"If he's that damned careless, he don't deserve to get it back," stated the third guard. "So let's us poor, deserving gentlemen share it between us."

Apparently the idea met with approval. Moving out of the light, the guards gathered in a bunch at the mouth of the alley and shared out the contents of the purse. With that done, they continued on their way discussing how they would spend their "lucky" find. Watching them pass from sight and listening to the sounds of their passing fading away, Hacker figured that another item of the plan had been successful. In possession of a twenty-dollar windfall each, the guards would be unlikely to hurry their return to the jail.

"That all of 'em, friend?" whispered a voice from behind Hacker.

Stifling a yelp of surprise, for he could have sworn that he had the alley to himself, Hacker whirled around and reached under his jacket. He could not see the speaker, so did not draw the Deringer concealed in the waistband of his trousers. Just as he decided that his ears had played a trick on him, he heard a faint chuckle and saw a slight movement at the rear of the bank.

"Who is it?" Hacker breathed.

"Kiowa," replied the tall, lean shape which came on noiseless feet from the shadows. "I'm Cap'n Fog's scout, mind me?"

"I do *now!*" Hacker answered. "You near on scared me white-haired."

"Didn't figure shouting, or singing 'Dixie' 'd be the thing to do," Kiowa drawled. "Have they all pulled out of the jail?"

"All the men have, I counted five of them," Hacker replied. "But the woman, the one they're using as matron, may still be there."

"Likely Cap'n Dusty can tend her needings if he has to," Kiowa said. "Now you'd best get going. I'll sort of keep watch down by the side of the jail house and stop any of those five yahoos coming back too early."

CHAPTER ELEVEN

You Ain't Killed Him, Have You?

"What the hell—?" gasped the guard who opened the door at Slasser's knock, staring at the sergeant's stew-smeared tunic. Then, seeing the anger on the three-bar's face, he stood aside and let them bring in their "prisoner." "Who've you got there, serge?"

Swiftly Dusty looked around and took note of his surroundings. They were standing in what must be the entrance hall of the building. Most of it was in darkness, but lamps illuminated the section by the side door through which he had entered. Off to his left, the stairs leading down to the basement were also well-lit. Men came from a room at the rear of the building. Four of them, wearing their hats and weapon belts like the one who had opened the door. Apparently the room served as their quarters, for Dusty could see two beds beyond its open door. The sergeant's wife who had been hired as a matron did not make her appearance.

Before Dusty could worry about the matron's non-appearance, Slasser thrust him into a chair by the table at the left of the door and snarled a warning that he had better stay put, or else! Having no intention of doing otherwise with the full complement of guards present, Dusty crouched in the chair trying to look terrified. His eyes went to the table. On it lay a pen, inkpot and the Guard Report Book in which details of prisoners accepted or discharged were entered.

"He's a stinking deserter is who," Slasser snarled. "And a real feisty one. Needs teaching proper respect for his betters and I reckon we're the boys to do it, don't you?"

Watching the men, Dusty saw that they understood the sergeant's meaning. He also read worry, concern and blank refusal on the coarse, hard faces. Even without knowing of Frost's and Wexler's intervention and interest in the small "prisoner," the five men wanted no part in the respect-teaching.

Self-preservation rather than common humanity caused their hesitation. Every one of the five enjoyed the privileges being a stockade guard brought and had no desire to be returned to their original regiments. They figured that it could happen if they took a part in beating up the small youngster.

Recently there had been incidents in which stockade guards had inflicted brutal beatings without cause on prisoners. Such things had always happened, of course, but the guards concerned had been careless. Their victims had been men with important friends. So word of their treatment had reached influential circles. Questions had been raised in Congress, while the "liberal" newspapers thundered demands for investigations and the prevention of further assaults. Such was the heat of public protest that the Union Army's top brass had given strict and definite orders to all Provost Marshals regarding the future conduct of the guards.

Dusty Fog possessed the supreme quality of a fighting cavalry officer, the ability to take advantage of any prevailing set of circumstances. Knowing something of the stockade situation, from conversations with captured Yankee soldiers and from Union newspapers gathered during raids, he had seen how they might make use of it. According to Wexler, Slasser had the reputation for being a sadistic brute who took pleasure in ill-treating prisoners. Such a man would not easily change his ways, no matter what instructions he received from the Provost Marshal. Especially if his temper could be roused in some way.

So the incident at the Birdcage Cafe had been planned; although Dusty had not expected the table to fall in such a satisfactory manner and was prepared to use feet or knees to achieve his end. Figuring that Slasser would then be determined to extract a savage revenge, Dusty had avoided stirring up the same desire on Pope's part. Wexler's "timely" arrival had been to ensure that the beating-up did not take place immediately, or out on the street. It had worked and Dusty found himself inside the jail-house. Now he was gambling on the other five guards being reluctant to endanger their careers by helping Slasser to work him over. If that happened, he felt sure the sergeant would be the more determined to do it without their assistance.

A very long, for Dusty at least, thirty seconds ticked by. The five guards shuffled their feet, exchanged glances with each other and Pope, but avoided meeting Slasser's cold eyes. Growing more impatient by the second, the sergeant unbuckled his belt and removed his tunic.

"What about it?" Slasser demanded, tossing the tunic on to the table and adjusting the belt about his middle. "Who's going to help me?"

This was the decisive moment. In a very short time Dusty would know if his rescue attempt stood any chance of succeeding—or whether he would be fighting for his life against the combined attack of several larger, heavier and stronger men all trained in rough-house self-defence.

Sure he and Wexler had made arrangements against the latter eventuality. If all had gone as it should, Hacker would have followed him to the jail and would carry a warning to the undertaker if the five guards did not leave within five minutes of his arrival. Maybe Wexler could not do his part by persuading Frost to visit the jail. Even if he did, they might arrive too late to save Dusty from injury.

"You know what the Man told us—" one of the five mumbled.

"The Man—!" Slasser spat out.

"He way out-ranks *you*," growled a surly-faced red-head who considered himself next in line for promotion. "So I ain't doing it!"

Looking at the others, Slasser saw that the blank refusal had caused them to make up their minds. All could remember the grim emphasis with which the Provost Marshal had spoken on the subject of mishandling prisoners. Unlike the sergeant, they had no cause to dislike the small "captive." So they all affirmed their non-compliance.

"Get the hell out of here, happen you feel that way!" Slasser snarled, face reddening with anger. "All of you can go."

"Come on, boys," said the red-head. "How about the food for that Reb gal?"

"It wasn't ready when we left the Birdcage," Pope answered. "One of you'll have to bring it with you."

"There's no call to rush back with it," Slasser continued, not wanting witnesses—particularly the red-haired corporal—around while he dealt with the small prisoner. "Where's Sarah?"

"She's gone home for the night," the red-head replied, making for the door. "If that gal wants anything, one of you'll have to tend to her."

With that, the men trooped out of the building. Pope closed and locked the door behind him, then turned with the expression of one who knew that he faced an unpleasant duty.

"Come on, Popey," Slasser said in a cajoling tone. "Let's put this short-growed son-of-a-bitch away for the night."

"It shouldn't take two of us," Pope answered, having been made extra wary by the refusal of the other five guards. "You take him down."

"What if he jumps me?" Slasser inquired.

"If that happens, it's between you and him," Pope replied. "I won't see it happen, but I'll take your word that's what he did."

"Have it your way," Slasser sniffed, knowing he could count on the corporal to give the right answer when questioned later. "I'll see to his needings."

With that he shot out his right hand to grip Dusty's collar. Jerking the small Texan out of the chair, he grinned a little. Hell, a runt like that would be easy meat. In fact two of them would probably reduce the fun by finishing him off too quickly. Catching Dusty's left wrist from underneath, Slasser deftly turned the trapped arm into a hammerlock position. The move was made with the swift ease of long practise. Experience had taught the sergeant that the combined hold was the best way for a single man to control and make a prisoner walk in a required direction.

Allowing himself to be guided to the wooden steps leading to the basement, Dusty kept alert without resisting. He was ready, if Slasser was to hurl him down the stairs, to try to break the force of his landing. Yet he doubted if the man would do so. Slasser wanted the pleasure of battering him to a pulp and to do it while he could still feel the blows landing.

So Dusty looked around him as he went down the stairs. Ahead of him, at the other side of the basement, were a line of ordinary open cells made out of steel bars. With a feeling of relief, he saw that they were unoccupied. No other prisoners had been brought in since Trumpeter released those already held to take part in the attack on the Snake Ford.

That raised the point of where the Yankees were holding Mrs. Greenhow. Once again Wexler had provided the answer. Turning his head to the right, Dusty studied the two rooms used to house female or dangerous male prisoners. Completely enclosed, they had solid wooden doors fitted with peep-holes and secured with double bolts but no locks. Only one of the doors had its bolts closed, so that would be the cell holding the Confederate lady spy.

Having satisfied himself on that score, Dusty gave thought to his escape. He could see well enough, for the basement was lit with hanging lamps. Once he reached the floor, he could make his move.

The moment Dusty felt the hard stone of the basement under his feet, he changed from passively yielding to dangerously active. Alert for the first warning sign, he was ready when Slasser slackened his grip ready to commence the beating. Instantly Dusty stepped back with his left foot, until it was alongside and pointing to the rear of the sergeant's right boot. Taking his weight on the right leg, Dusty pivoted his body to the left and used its motion to free his trapped arm. Before Slasser had become fully aware of the danger, Dusty drew the bent arm from behind his back. Snapping it upwards and twisting his palm to face his assailant, he pulled the wrist from the other's fingers.

Up to that point Dusty had displayed only a frightened, unresisting obedience. So the sudden transition to aggression took Slasser completely by surprise. Having already loosened his hold, he could not prevent the trapped wrist from slipping out of his grasp. Instinctively he tightened his grip on the collar, which was what Dusty wanted him to do. Pressing his left forearm and shoulder against Slasser's right arm, Dusty used the leverage he exerted to throw the other off balance. While he could not apply sufficient pressure to throw the sergeant to the floor, Dusty opened the way for a continuation of the attack. Drawing back his right arm, Dusty ripped a punch into his captor's solar plexus. Due to his own awkward position, he could not strike with his full power. The blow landed hard enough to bring a grunt of pain from its recipient. While it also caused him to release Dusty's collar and take an involuntary step to the rear, it did not incapacitate him.

Swiftly Dusty brought up his right foot in a stamping kick aimed at Slasser's body. Showing considerable speed for so bulky a man, the sergeant snapped his hands down and caught the rising leg by its ankle. With a twisting heave, he pitched Dusty across the basement. Slasser failed to appreciate that his efforts alone did not cause the small Texan's flight through the air. Feeling his ankle trapped and the first warning twist at it, Dusty applied a counter learned from Tommy Okasi. Thrusting up with his other leg, he added force to the sergeant's heave and went with it. Long training at *ju-jitsu* and riding had taught Dusty how to fall on even hard surfaces. Covering his head with his forearms, he curled his body into a ball and lit down rolling. The wall halted his progress and he used it to force himself upright.

"Try to escape, would you?" Slasser roared, loud enough for the words to reach Pope so that they could be repeated later as "proof" that he had acted in self-defense.

Something about Dusty's attitude as he rose warned

Slasser of danger. No other prisoner had managed to escape from the collar-and-hammerlock take-down hold. Yet the small man had done so— Or was he small? Standing in that half-crouched position of readiness, he gave the impression of size and deadly, latent power. Maybe he called for stronger measures than mere bare hands.

Sliding the baton from its belt loop, Slasser gripped it in his right hand and moved forward. He looked as big as a bull buffalo, dangerous as a winter-starved grizzly bear and meaner than a stick-teased diamondback rattlesnake. Rushing forward, he revised his opinion. Despite the quick way in which he made his feet, the small "deserter" seemed dazed and unready to resist. Disinclined to take chances, but not wanting his victim to lose consciousness too quickly, Slasser raised the baton. Down it whistled in a blow calculated to strike Dusty's collarbone and either break it or leave it numbly inoperative.

Although Dusty looked dazed, he had never been more alert. Guessing what his attacker intended, he waited until the club began its downwards swing before thrusting himself sideways along the wall. Swinging around before Slasser regained control of the baton, Dusty snapped another side-kick. His boot thudded against Slasser's right bicep, but not hard enough to put the muscle out of action. Knowing better than to go in close, Dusty made no other attack. He wanted room to manoeuvre, so sprang away from the wall and turned ready to take the offensive.

Once again Slasser displayed his speed. Swivelling in a fast turn, he spat a curse and lunged towards the small Texan. Out licked the club, in a round-house swing powerful enough to crush Dusty's skull if it had landed. It missed, but the sergeant whipped it across in a snapping back-hand slash directed at the side of Dusty's head. While launching it, Slasser reached a decision. Much as he hated to admit it, the small "captive" was proving too much for him.

"Pope!" the sergeant bawled at the top of his voice. "Get the he—!"

Realizing the danger, Dusty moved in. He shot his left

foot out to the left, bending his right leg and ducking his head and torso underneath the arc of the baton's swing. Feeling the wind of the stout oak club's passing stir his hair, he flung up his left hand to block and hold off its return. Hearing Slasser start to shout, he knew that he must finish the sergeant before Pope put in an appearance. It seemed that providence had offered him a way of doing so.

In turning, Slasser had halted with his feet spread apart. From his crouching posture, adopted to evade the blow, Dusty was ideally placed to take the advantage offered to him. Drawing back his right fist, he propelled it foward and, this time, was in a perfect position to strike. Driving up with the full force of the small but powerful frame behind them, his knuckles smashed into Slasser's testicles.

Numbing agony tore at the burly non-com. It was a torment that numbed the mind and tore into his vital organs. Chopping off, the yell for help turned into a croaking bawl of anguish. The baton fell from his limp fingers and he was helpless, unable to think of defending himself against Dusty's next actions. For, wanting to render the sergeant *hors de combat* before Pope arrived the small Texan did not content himself with merely striking the blow.

From impacting on Slasser's lower body, Dusty's right hand flashed up to join the left. They both closed on the trapped wrist, turning the sergeant's hand palm-upwards. At the same time Dusty spun on his heel so that he stood with his back to Slasser. Levering the arm against its elbow joint, Dusty bent his torso forward and catapulted the man over his shoulder. Turning in the air, he came down hard on to the stone floor. Dusty thought that he heard the pop of breaking bones as Slasser landed. It was a sound that would have gladdened the hearts of many prisoners who had suffered under the burly sergeant's baton, boots and hard fists.

Following Slasser down, Dusty noticed that his head tilted over at an unnatural angle. The sound he had heard must have been caused by the other's neck breaking. Jerking open Slasser's holster, Dusty slid the revolver from it.

He could not remember when the smooth, hand-fitting curves of an Army Colt's butt had last felt so comforting. The sergeant was out of the deal, but that did not mean the game had been won. Dusty still had Pope to deal with; a point very quickly brought home.

"Did you shout, serge?" called the corporal from the hall above.

All too well Dusty knew what that meant. When no answer came and Pope could not hear the sounds of Slasser working on the prisoner, he was certain to investigate. So Dusty looked around for a way in which he might silence the second guard. Although he had taken Slasser's revolver, it did not supply the answer. The sound of a shot might be heard outside the building. Nor did hiding in the main line of cells present a better solution; their barred walls offered no concealment. For a moment Dusty thought of hiding in the room next to where he hoped to find Rose Greenhow. The trouble being that it was the obvious place for him to go.

"What's doing down there?" asked Pope, sounding a mite worried.

Figuring that time was running out, Dusty saw the ideal hiding-place and wondered why he had not thought of it straight away. Darting across to the stairs, he ducked into the triangular cavity beneath them. Used to store the jail's brooms and buckets, the space was large enough for his purposes. More than that, the wooden steps had no fronts. Dusty found that he could see and, more important, reach through the gaps between the steps.

Almost as soon as he had taken his place, he heard Pope's footsteps drawing nearer. Slipping the Colt into his waistband to leave both hands free, he drew in a deep breath and let it out gently.

"You ain't killed him, have you?" the corporal demanded anxiously, sounding almost directly above the waiting Texan. "If you have, I'd— What the hell—?"

Clearly Pope had just received his first view of Slasser's sprawled-out body. Dusty wondered what he made of it. Expecting that he would find Slasser standing over the still, possibly lifeless, figure of their "prisoner," learning that the sergeant was the victim must have come as a hell of a shock. The footsteps halted as Pope took in the scene. Faintly Dusty heard the rasp of steel on leather, which meant that the corporal had drawn his revolver, and he waited for the sound of its hammer going back to full cock. The feet resumed their movement without it coming. Either Pope had forgotten a basic precaution, or he held a double-action weapon which did not require cocking before it could be fired. Whichever reason applied, the corporal came down the stairs at a good speed.

"Keep moving, damn you!" Dusty breathed, hands raising towards the gap on a level with his eyes. "Don't start figuring out where I'm at!"

Almost as if he had heard and was willing to oblige, Pope continued to hurry down the stairs. Remembering the small size of their prisoner and his apparently meek acceptance of capture, the corporal was astonished by what lay below. Not until half-way to the bottom did he start to realize that he could not locate the second party in the drama.

The realization came just a moment too late.

Seeing Pope's right foot descend on to the step in front of him, Dusty reached through the gap with both hands. Already stepping forward with his other leg, the corporal felt his leading ankle seized in a powerful grip but could not stop himself advancing. Jerking back hard on the captured limb, Dusty contrived to throw Pope off balance. With the corporal's wail of shock and terror ringing in his ears, Dusty opened his hands. Carried forward by his impetus, Pope hit a lower step with one foot then pitched on across the basement.

Released by its owner, the revolver sailed through the air. Hardly daring to breathe, Dusty watched its flight towards the cells. It landed on the floor, bounced and struck one of the doors but did not fire.

With no control of his limbs, Pope landed erect and continued to move. Flailing desperately, his arms tried to grab at the air in an attempt to stop himself, but to no avail.

Still travelling fast, he crashed head-first into a cell. The top of his skull rammed against one of the steel bars with a sickening thud and he crumpled limply on top of his revolver.

Dusty leapt from the cavity, running towards Pope. Although he went prepared to use boots or hands to complete the silencing, he saw that neither would be necessary. Blood and something grey were oozing from the corporal's head, spreading evilly on the floor. The way had been opened for Dusty to set Rose Greenhow free.

CHAPTER TWELVE

They've Taken All My Clothes

Satisfied that he need not worry himself further about the two guards, Dusty still took precautions. Raising Pope's unresisting body, he retrieved the revolver from beneath it. He examined the gun, recognizing it as a double-action Starr Army model; which explained why the impact against the bars had not caused it to fire. However the force of the collision had damaged the base-pin and thrown the cylinder out of line, so it would be of no use to him.

Dropping the revolver, Dusty rose and crossed the room. Glancing at the stairs, he drew back the bolts and opened the door behind which he hoped to find Rose Greenhow. Light flooded into the small cell, giving Dusty his first view of the woman he had risked his life to rescue. She stood in the centre of the cubicle, blinking a little but tense and alert.

"Who are you?" she demanded in a voice as brittle with menace as the spitting snarl of a she-bobcat preparing to defend its young.

In her mid-thirties, Rose Greenhow was a tall woman with a statuesque, magnificently curved figure. Dusty was left in no doubt on that score. Her milk-white shoulders and arms were naked as she hugged at the coarse grey U.S. Army blanket wrapped around her torso. Ending at knee-level, leaving her perfectly-formed bare legs and feet exposed to his gaze, it emphasized the swell of her bosom, slender waist and richly contoured hips. Black hair, some-what dishevelled at that moment, framed a strikingly beautiful face with proud, defiant, hazel eyes. Surprise showed on her patrician features as she stared at him, mingled with suspicion but giving no hint of fear.

"Captain Fog, Texas Light Cavalry, ma'am," Dusty replied and as Wexler had warned him that she would want proof that he was speaking the truth, went on, "Simon Oakland helped me to get in here so that I could rescue you."

"I don't know what you mean," the woman declared, looking at the small, insignificant youngster in the ill-fitting civilian clothes. "In fact, I still don't know why I have been subjected to this scandalous treatment. When my husband hears what has happened—"

Nothing about her showed that she recognized the name of the man who was to have made contact with her and helped her to reach Ole Devil Hardin. In fact, despite speaking with the accent of a well-bred Southern lady, she sounded genuine in her reaction. There was one thing that made Dusty sure that he had not made a mistake. Clearly she had been disturbed by the sounds of the fight in the basement, even if she could not see it. Looking behind him, her eyes took in the two motionless guards sprawled on the floor. If she was, as she claimed, the wife of a Yankee officer imprisoned by mistake, she ought to be screeching her head off for help.

"We've no time to waste, ma'am," he warned, drawing the Colt from his waist-band and offering it butt forward to her. "It's full-capped and loaded. Can you use it?"

Despite her caution, Rose Greenhow desperately wanted to believe a rescue bid was in progress. Yet she knew that the Yankee Secret Service might be trying to trick her. Looking from the revolver to Dusty, she thought fast. If the enemy had faked the escape, they would have selected a more credible "rescuer;" one whose stature made him capable of felling the pair of guards. The small man had said he was Captain Fog of the Texas Light Cavalry. He spoke like a well-educated Texan, and she had heard stories of Dusty Fog's bare-hand fighting prowess. Everything depended on his response to her next words.

"I leave such violent things to my cousin," she said, not touching the gun.

"Oakland allows that Miss Boyd's real good with that fancy *ivory*-handled *Navy* revolver *David* Dance made up special for her," Dusty answered, knowing that he was facing a test and supplying the information given to him by Wexler.

All Rose's suspicions went as she listened to the emphasis Dusty placed on certain words. While a Yankee might guess which cousin she had meant, the small Texan knew the maker, type and furnishings of Belle Boyd's revolver. That information could only have come from somebody deep in the Confederate States' Secret Service. The details he had given were not of the kind which might have been extracted under torture from a captured spy.

So she accepted Dusty as genuine. Then she saw the quizzical manner with which he was studying her. Thinking fast, she realized that one of his facts had not been entirely correct. Only a small thing. It could have been a mistake—or he might be doing a little testing on his own account.

"David Dance may have carved the handle," she said. "But it was George who made the gun."

"Yes, ma'am," Dusty agreed. "David's the woodworker of the family."

"I'm sorry, Captain," Rose went on. "In my line of work one takes few things at their face value."

"It's a good way to be, ma'am. I'm a mite that way myself," Dusty drawled, confirming her suspicion that the wrong name had been deliberate. "I've settled the guards, but their *amigos* might come back any time. We'd best get moving."

"That won't be easy," Rose pointed out, gesturing at the blanket. "They've taken all my clothes."

"The hell you say!" Dusty ejaculated. "That's one thing me and Wex—Oakland never figured on. Do you reckon they're upstairs in the guards' quarters?"

"I doubt it. When that Yankee pig of a Provost Marshal had me stripped, he said he would take my clothes to headquarters and make a thorough examination of them. Much good that will do him. All my information is in my head."

At that moment Dusty was not greatly interested in how Rose carried her information. Silently he cursed the lack of foresight which had caused them to overlook the possibility of the Yankees taking Rose's clothes. All too well he realized the difficult position her state of undress placed them in. Maybe the blanket served to retain some semblance of her modesty, but it would be completely inadequate for what lay ahead. Even if she could walk barefooted and unnoticed through the back-streets, it would be impossible for her to make the long, hard, fast ride to safety clad in such a manner. Nor could Wexler help. Wanting him to have as good an alibi as possible, Dusty had arranged to head for the Ouachita without meeting him again. Wexler would spend the time until the escape was discovered in the company of Frost, so Dusty could not contact him.

As Rose joined him at the cell's door, Dusty looked around the basement in search of inspiration. His eyes went to the two motionless shapes on the floor, then swung speculatively back to the woman. From what he read on Rose's face, her thoughts were running along similar lines to his own.

"Can you use this, ma'am?" Dusty inquired, offering her the Colt again.

"If I have to."

"Then take it and watch the stairs. I'll get you something to wear. Which I sure hope you're not a choosy dresser, ma'am."

"That depends on what I'm dressing for," Rose smiled, wondering how she had ever thought of her rescuer as being small. "I'm sure that I can manage with what you have in mind, under the circumstances."

Taking the revolver from Dusty's hands, Rose watched him cross the room. Pausing for a moment, he studied the two men and decided that Pope—being slightly smaller than Slasser—was the better suited to his needs. At that the corporal's clothing would be far too large for Rose, but they had nothing else for her to wear. Glancing over his shoulder, Dusty saw that she had turned her attention to the stairs. Grim determination creased the beautiful face and she handled the Colt with calm competence as her ears strained to catch any warning sounds which came from the entrance hall.

Knowing that he could rely on the woman to keep a good watch, Dusty knelt at Pope's side and started to undress him. With a wry, distasteful twist to his lips, he unfastened the rawhide laces and removed the ankle-length Jefferson-pattern shoes. Under them Pope had on a pair of almost new, thick grey woollen socks far superior to the usual stove-pipe* variety issued by the Quartermasters' Department. Taking them off, he thrust them into the shoes and unbuckled the baton-loaded belt. Then he raised Pope into a sitting position, leaning him against the bars of the cell, trying to prevent the blood from running on to the tunic.

Leaving Dusty to work without interruption, Rose maintained her watch on the stairs. Nothing happened to alarm her and at last the small Texan stood up. Carrying a bundle of clothes and a pair of shoes in his arms, he rejoined her. Rose could not hold down a smile as he approached. In addition to the Union-blue coloured garments which she had expected, she noticed one of red flannel material. Glancing by Dusty, she discovered that Pope lay as naked as she had been before wrapping herself in the blanket. Turning her eyes back to her rescuer, she was surprised to see him blushing.

"They're not the clothes for a lady, ma'am," Dusty apologized. "Only it'll be a rough ride back to our lines and I figured you'd need them."

"Anything will be a welcome improvement, Captain," Rose assured him. "Will you put them on the bed for me, please?"

"Sure, ma'am," Dusty agreed.

---

*So called due to their alleged resemblance in shape to the elbow of a stove-pipe and because after about forty-eight hours' wear the socks, like the pipe, had a hole at each end.

"Then, if you'll keep watch, I'll dress as quickly as I can," Rose continued, wiping off her smile so as to avoid embarrassing him.

Entering the cell, Dusty dumped his burden on the bunk. Almost snatching the revolver from Rose's hand, he scuttled through the door. She smiled, wondering if the threat of armed enemies would have made him depart so hurriedly. Still smiling, she dropped the blanket and picked up the long-legged red flannel drawers.

None of the clothing fitted her, which came as no surprise. The trousers hung baggily, but with the suspenders tightened and waist-belt taken to its last notch, they stayed in place. Even with the thick socks on, the ends of the trouser legs tucked into the uppers and the laces drawn as tight as she could manage, she felt that she had her feet inside a couple of packing boxes. However the shoes served their purpose and ought to stay on unless she tried to be to active.

"How the mighty have fallen," Rose sighed ruefully as she buttoned the loose-fitting tunic, thinking back to the days when she had been known as the best-dressed hostess in Washington's glittering social whirl. "I'd hate for Cousin Belle to see me like this."

Shuffling from the cell, she joined Dusty at the foot of the stairs. In passing, she noticed that he had taken the time to find a blanket and had covered Pope with it.

"You sure look elegant, ma'am," Dusty grinned, looking at her and holding out the corporal's weapon-belt with the baton hanging from it. "There's only one last touch needed. There's no revolver, but I'd keep the club if I was you."

"Yes, it will help my disguise," Rose agreed. "I should imagine that ordinary soldiers try to avoid stockade guards. So if any of them see it, they won't come too close. What I need now is a hat."

"Pope must've left his upstairs," Dusty suggested. "Let's go and look."

The entrance hall was deserted when they reached it. Leaving Rose to collect that hat, Dusty made for the side door. He intended to look outside, but the open Guard Report Book caught his eye. Thinking of what Wexler had told him about Trumpeter's reaction to his activities, Dusty started to smile. If any member of Company "C" had seen that smile, they would have known that their leader was planning some fresh devilment to torment the Yankees. Sliding the Colt into his waistband, he went to the table.

Tucking stray curls under the brim of a Burnside campaign hat she had found, Rose emerged from the guards' room. She saw Dusty return the pen to the inkpot and straighten up from the table. Wondering what he had been doing, she joined him. A gurgle of delight broke from her as she looked at the book. While waiting, he had filled in the section marked *REASON FOR ARREST OR RELEASE*.

"To be returned to her loved ones," Rose read, "by order of General Jackson Baines Hardin, C.S.A. Signed, D.E.M. Fog, Captain, Texas Light Cavalry." While amused, she felt that she should give a warning. "Trumpeter will be fit to be tied when he sees this."

"Likely, ma'am," Dusty admitted. "Which's why I've done it. A man in a temper's judgment gets clouded. He quits thinking straight and acts rash. So I want for him to know who rescued you."

"He'll still realize that you must have had local help."

"Yes, ma'am. Only, way he feels about me already, I'm figuring he'll be wanting *me* even worse than the fellers who helped."

"Trumpeter's a vindictive, vicious man, Captain Fog. There's no telling what he might do to take his revenge on you. Take care in future and *don't* fall into his hands."

"I'll try extra hard not to, ma'am," Dusty promised and took the key from the lock.

Opening the door, Dusty looked out. Nobody was in sight, so they left the building. Wanting to make things look as normal as possible, he closed and locked the door behind them. Then they walked along the alley towards the rear of the building. Just as they passed through the light thrown by the guards' room's window, they heard footsteps behind them.

"Hold it up there, corporal!" barked an authoritative voice.

Looking back, Rose saw two men at the mouth of the alley. She recognized both of them. The one in the uniform of a Union Army captain and carrying a bundle wrapped in a blanket was the Provost Marshal. At his side, looking a mite distressed and perturbed, waddled Hoffinger.

"Best do what they say, ma'am," Dusty whispered. "If we run now, they'll raise the alarm. Let them come real close."

Slipping free the baton as she turned, Rose held it concealed at her side. Dusty had not drawn the Colt after filling in the column of the book, but made no atempt to touch it. Everything depended on them retaining the element of surprise. They stood far enough beyond the window's light to be indistinct shapes rather than identifiable figures. Given just a smidgin of good Texas luck, the approaching men would not discover their mistake until close enough for him to deal silently with them.

"Where're you going and what's that kid doing around here?" the captain demanded, striding unsuspectingly towards what he assumed to be one of the stockade guards and a local youngster.

Looking at the figures, Hoffinger felt a growing, uneasy suspicion that one of them seemed familiar. Not the corporal, although there was something odd about "him," but the civilian. For some reason, the way the smaller shape stood facing them appeared to strike a chord in Hoffinger's memory.

Small!

That was the word needed to trigger off the dude's realization of the truth. Dusty Fog had stood in just such a manner, apparently relaxed but at coil-spring readiness, just before launching his attack on Glock.

"It's DusTY FO—!" Hoffinger yelped, his voice rising higher as the certainty of the suspicion grew.

The recognition had not come quickly enough. Already the two men were in the darkness beyond the window and close to the waiting couple. Although it had been Dusty's intention to silence the Provost Marshal first, he changed his mind in a hurry. Hoffinger must be prevented from making any more noise.

Mentally cursing the lousy turn of fate that had brought the chubby dude to the jail-house, Dusty sprang forward. With the speed that allowed him to draw and shoot a Colt in less than a second, his right hand stabbed in Hoffinger's direction. A thumb and four powerful fingers closed about the dude's throat, sinking in and tightening with a force that paralysed his vocal cord. Even as Hoffinger's words chopped off, Dusty's left hand reached for the Colt in his waistband ready to deal with the Yankee officer.

The need did not arise. For a refined, well-bred Southern lady, Rose showed a remarkably quick grasp of the situation and moved with commendable speed. Seeing Dusty leap at and silence the dude, she devoted herself to the Provost Marshal. In fact, recalling the humiliation suffered at his hands during the search and removal or her clothing, she found satisfaction in being given the chance to settle accounts with him.

Bringing up the baton, she lunged and drove its tip hard into his solar plexus. With a croak of pain, he dropped the bundle and jerked backwards. Rose followed him, swinging the baton around. Crashing on to the captain's head, which was encased in a silk-braided fatigue cap, the blow tumbled him to the ground.

"And Cousin Belle couldn't have done it neater," Rose told herself. Then, hearing a sound from the rear of the alley, she turned with the baton lifting to strike.

Dragging the croaking Hoffinger after him at arm's length, Dusty also turned. He recognized the tall, lean shape looming through the blackness and spoke a warning, "Don't hit him, ma'am. He's one of mine."

Judging by his captain's tone that some explanation of his presence might be called for, Kiowa decided to avoid making it if he could. Instead he acted as if he had been obeying orders.

"Thought I heard somebody coming 'round the back, Cap'n Dusty. It was only a cat when I got there."

With a heave, Dusty propelled the half-strangled Hoffinger towards the scout. Catching the front of the dude's jacket in his left hand, Kiowa held the point of his knife to the centre of the fancy vest.

"Keep him quiet!" Dusty ordered. "How's the captain, Mrs. Greenhow?"

"He looks better now than when we last met," she replied and the tension she felt made her continue. "For the Good Lord's sake call me 'Rose.' You make me feel old, saying 'ma'am' and 'Mrs.' "

"Yes, m—Rose," Dusty grinned, looking at the Provost Marshal and deciding he would be no danger for some time. "Let's go."

"How about him, Cap'n?" Kiowa inquired, shaking Hoffinger who was too busy trying to recover from the strangling grip to protest.

For a moment Dusty hesitated and Hoffinger's life hung in the balance. If Dusty had given the word, Kiowa would have driven his knife home. Two things saved the chubby dude, Dusty's aversion to cold-blooded, unnecessary killing and the fact that he saw a way of making use of the man.

"Bring him with us," Dusty ordered. "But if he tries to make fuss, or shout to anybody, kill him."

"That's easy enough done," drawled Kiowa, deftly twirling his captive towards the rear of the building. Transferring his hold to the back of Hoffinger's coat collar, he pricked the bowie knife at the spot where its blade could most easily reach the kidneys. "Start your feet moving, *hombre*. Do like Cap'n Dusty says or I'll leave you here permanent."

Remembering Kiowa as vividly as Dusty from their last encounter, Hoffinger did not doubt that he would obey his captain's order. So he had no intention of causing trouble, or trying to warn any members of the garrison they chanced to meet that Rose Greenhow had escaped.

"This's the Provost Marshal, Dusty," Rose remarked, stirring the unconscious officer with her toe. "Perhaps he was coming to collect me."

"Or set you free, figuring it was all a mistake," Dusty answered, picking up the bundle. "This feels like it's got clothes and shoes in it."

"They'd know Hoffinger didn't make a mistake," Rose told him. "There was a knife-bracelet and a ring that would tell them who I am. Come on, we'd better get away from here."

An unprotesting Hoffinger allowed himself to be hustled through the back streets. Nobody saw the party and they reached the outskirts without being challenged. As he walked, he wondered why Dusty had ordered that he be brought along. Not to be killed that could have been done just as easily by the jail-house and was against the small Texan's chivalrous nature. Certainly not as a hostage, to be traded for their freedom if they were caught. Dusty Fog, and more particularly Rose Greenhow, knew the Yankees would never make such a *trade*.

"Why have you brought him, Dusty?" Rose inquired and Hoffinger listened with interest. "Will you release him when we get to the horses?"

"No, ma—Rose. I'm going to take him with us to Prescott."

"Because he denounced me to the Yankees? If so, I assure you that I've no desire for revenge. It was my own fault that I was recognized. I felt so sure that nobody in Arkansas would recognize me that I didn't travel in disguise."

"Revenge's not what I'm figuring on. Like you said at the jail-house, Trumpeter's going to know I had help from somebody in Little Rock. So I'm fixing to let him know who it was."

"I don't—" Rose began, then gasped out, "Hoffinger!"

"Yes'm. There's going to be a rumour started that he's one of our spies. Old Trumpeter's going to be reminded of a few lil things. Like how we knew where to find the remounts and how we come to be on the Snake Ford at just the right time after we'd met Hoffinger. Time we're through, Trumpeter'll be certain that Hoffinger's been working for us all along."

"You've hit it!" Rose enthused. "He'll even think that Hoffinger denouncing me was part of a plot to make him look foolish when I escaped. He's egotistical enough to accept that we'd do it just to have him removed from command, for fear of his brilliance."

Listening, Hoffinger felt a shudder run through him. Once those rumours started to circulate, he was a doomed man in Little Rock. Remembering Trumpeter's delight at capturing the notorious Rose Greenhow, he could imagine the reaction when the general heard of her escape. Hoffinger's disappearance would seem like conclusive proof of guilt. Ironically, he had asked to accompany the Provost Marshal, on hearing that the officer intended to interrogate Rose, hoping that his presence would prevent her from being brutally ill-treated. Not that his good intentions— even if Trumpeter had known about them—would save him. The general would show him no mercy. In fact Trumpeter would not want him taken alive so that he could testify to how he had deceived the most brilliant brain in the Union Army.

"Fetching him along's going to slow us down some, Cap'n Dusty," Kiowa warned. "We don't have a relay for him to use and we're late starting back as it is."

A point which Dusty had been considering since deciding how to use Hoffinger. The need for speed had prevented him from bringing more than the bare minimum of horses for his party. Rescuing Rose had consumed valuable hours that ought to have been spent in heading for the safety of the Ouachita River. Expecting to start back almost immediately, he had planned the journey accordingly. Slowed down by being unable to use the full potential of the two-horse relays, dawn would find them far from the wooded country where he had hoped that they could hide during the day. However he had to balance that against the chance to remove all suspicion from Wexler. Dusty thought that the opportunity justified the risk.

"We'll take a chance on it," he told the others.

CHAPTER THIRTEEN

He's Left Me Afoot So's He Can Escape

Just as Dusty feared, sun-up found them traversing rolling but open country. So they kept moving, with Kiowa ranging ahead of them, keeping to the low land and avoiding sky-lines if they could.

On rejoining his men, Dusty had changed back into his uniform. The bundle had held Rose's clothing, but she retained the borrowed outfit except for donning her own shoes. Everything had been ready for their departure. Pausing only long enough to tell Hacker—who had met Dusty's group on the edge of town—of the scheme to incriminate Hoffinger, they had moved out. The alarm bell had sounded before they had covered a mile, warning them that Rose's escape had been discovered. No pursuit came close, nor could the news be passed ahead. Seeing Dusty returning with Rose, Sandy McGraw had found and cut the telegraph line to the south-west.

Towards noon they were travelling along the bottom of a large valley. Ahead of them, Kiowa peered cautiously over the rim of the left-hand slope. Ducking down his head, he turned his horse and galloped back to his companions.

"There's a Yankee patrol coming this way, Cap'n Dusty," the scout announced. "Once they top that rim, they'll see us for sure."

"No place to hide, either," Dusty replied, looking around. "How many of them and how far off are they?"

"Twenty or so, look like 3rd Cavalry to me. About half a mile off."

"Too many to fight," Dusty decided. "There's only one

chance. I'm going to make a stab at drawing them away from you."

"You?" Rose gasped.

"Yes'm. I haven't ridden my black all night and I'll bet he's got the legs of any horse in the Yankee Army. When they see me, they'll give chase—Especially if they know who I am."

"That's for sure," Kiowa growled, for Dusty had passed on Wexler's information during the night. "After Trumpeter putting out that order about you, every blue-belly officer in Arkansas'd give his right arm for a chance to get you."

"How can you be sure they'll recognize you, Dusty?" Rose inquired.

"Vern's going to tell them," Dusty answered. "If you'll do it, Vern, that is. Could be you'll wind up in a Yankee prison-camp—"

"Allus did want to see what one of them looked like," the old corporal drawled laconically. "Just what've you got in mind?"

Quickly Dusty explained his scheme. Watching the men, Rose saw that they showed no hesitation in accepting it. Even Hassle, who might end up as a prisoner-of-war, gave his agreement.

"How about Hoffinger?" Rose asked.

"Have no fear, dear lady," the dude answered. "By this time I am branded as a Confederate spy. My life depends on reaching your side of the Ouachita River. I will do nothing to impede our escape."

"See you don't," Dusty ordered. "Go with Kiowa, Rose. And Kiowa, *you* keep going no matter what happens to us."

Leading a twenty-strong patrol of the 3rd Cavalry, 1st Lieutenant Koebel saw a rider coming over the ridge up which he and his men were about to ascend. Even as Koebel realized that the newcomer was a Confederate cavalry captain, a second figure followed him. On foot, the man wore the uniform of a Texas Light Cavalry corporal. He was short, white-haired and clearly very angry.

"Come back with the hoss, blast ye!" the old corporal screeched, bounding after the captain.

Suddenly the Confederate officer became aware of the 3rd Cavalry patrol's presence. Reining his horse in a tight turn, he let out a yell, raked it with his spurs and sent it racing away at a tangent to the north-east. The corporal drew his right hand revolver, firing a shot in the direction of his departing superior.

"Take six men and get after him, sergeant!" Koebel barked. "Remainder, draw pistols and follow me."

While his sergeant gave chase to the fleeing captain, Koebel led the rest of the patrol up the slope. From all appearances, the old Rebel non-com was too filled with indignation at the officer's disertion to see the danger.

"Blast your stinking hide, Cap'n Fog!" the corporal bellowed in a carrying voice. "You come back here!"

Until he heard the name spoken by the furious old-timer, Koebel had intended to go over the rim and see if more of the enemy were in the vicinity. Instead he brought his horse to a rump-scraping halt. His men also stopped their mounts, amused by the ancient Rebel's antics.

"Who did you say he was?" Koebel demanded, hoping that he had heard correctly. "Who is he?"

Glaring around him, Vern Hassle howled in well-simulated exasperation and flung down his smoking revolver. Although his right holster was empty, the discarded Colt had belonged to Slasser. Stamping his feet in a paroxysm of wrath, he shook his fists in the air.

"Blast that Dusty Fog's hide!" Hassle raged. "He's left me afoot so's he can escape."

"Was that *Dusty* Fog?" asked one of the soldiers.

"Of course it b—!" Vern began, then stared wildly around as if the true nature of his position had just struck him. "Now look what he's done! I knowed I shouldn't've come on this scout with him!"

Ignoring the excited chatter which rose from his men, Koebel hurriedly revised his plans. To hell with going over the rim, there would be nothing on the other side. It was obvious what had happened. Fog had somehow lost his horse while on a mission accompanied only by the corporal. Typical of an arrogant Southerner, he had taken the aged non-com's mount. On seeing the patrol, Fog had deserted his companion and fled. If the rest of his Company had been close by, he would have attacked instead of running.

While there might be gaps in Koebel's logic, he refused to see them. From all he had heard, whoever captured or killed Dusty Fog would stand high in General Trumpeter's favour. The man responsible could expect promotion and further recognition from the grateful commanding general —and Koebel had sent his sergeant after the fleeing Rebel instead of going himself.

"Guard this feller, corporal, you two men!" Koebel ordered, the words tumbling out in his haste to get started. "Come on, the rest of you. After him. I'll give a month's pay to the man who brings him down."

Already primed with excitement, the soldiers needed no further encouragement. Setting their horses into motion, they galloped at a reckless pace towards the rest of their party. Watching them go, the Yankee corporal gave a disgusted sniff and swung from his saddle.

"Rest your butt-ends," he told his companions. "They've got a long ride ahead of them. Shed the gunbelt, old timer."

"Won't I just!" Hassle answered, complying. "To hell with fighting for the South, happens that's how an officer treats me!"

"All officers're sons-of-bitches," grinned one of the privates, holstering his Colt as he dismounted. "Look how Koebel's rid off and left us."

"I hope he enjoys the ride," the second soldier remarked, dropping his gun into leather as he watched the chase. " 'Cause I'm betting that's all he gets. That hoss of Fog's runs like a pronghorn antelope in a hurry."

"Fog's hoss!" Hassle yelped. "That's *my* danged hoss!"

And, tossing his gunbelt to the Yankee corporal, he launched into a magnificently profane discourse on the subject of Dusty's behaviour, morals, ancestry and possible fate. All in all it proved to be a fine performance and the Yankees listened with considerable amusement, not noticing that the rest of the patrol went rushing away from them. Hassle watched the departure, straining his inventive powers to find ways to keep his guards occupied. At last he paused for breath, standing snorting like a mossy-horned bull.

"That's was sure beautiful to hear," chuckled one of the privates. "It'll be a real pity to waste you on them prison-camps' guards."

"Danged if I ain't pleased to be going to one," Hassle answered, rubbing his hips. "Trouble being, I've drawed on next month's pay and 'twouldn't be right not to go back and work it out."

"Don't see as you've any other choice, pop," the Yankee corporal said, letting the barrel of his Colt dangle downwards and shaking Hassle's gunbelt.

Still rubbing at his sides, the old timer moved his hands behind his back in a casual-seeming manner.

"Could argue about that, son," he said and the right hand appeared holding the second of his revolvers which had been tucked into the back of his breeches. Cocking the hammer, he threw down on the other two-bar and continued, "Let it drop peaceable. I'm mortal bound to dee-cline your offer."

"And I'm here to see he gets that chance!" Sandy McGraw announced, rising from the top of the slope with Dusty's Henry rifle aimed at the Yankee privates.

Staring into the muzzle of the old Dragoon Colt, the Yankee corporal stood still. Before he could line his revolver, the Dragoon would put lead into him. He flickered a glance at and estimated the rest of the patrol were too far away to hear the sound of shooting over the thunder of their horses' hooves. Then he looked at his companions. Faced with a Henry repeater, they showed no inclination to take chances.

All of the trio had served long enough in Arkansas to know of the Texas Light Cavalry's skill with firearms and chivalrous treatment of prisoners. Deciding that they would be killed if they resisted, but released unharmed should they surrender, they followed the sensible course. Letting his revolver and Hassle's gun-belt drop to the ground, the corporal joined his companions in raising their arms.

"I reckon we've been slickered," the corporal said, eyeing Hassle with a mixture of annoyance and admiration. "Now what?"

"Soon's we've took your guns, you boys can get going," the old timer replied. "We wouldn't want you to be toting all that extry weight while you're walking—Which you will be. We'll be needing your hosses."

"So'll you be walking, for a long spell, happen Cap'n Dusty gets to know what you called him," Sandy declared, feeling relieved.

If the ruse had failed, he would have started shooting in an attempt at preventing the patrol from crossing the rim. So would Vern, while Dusty turned and charged to the attack. In that event, their chances of survival would have been slight.

Holding his black stallion to a gallop, Dusty turned in the saddle to see if his scheme was working. To his satisfaction, he found that the second portion of the patrol had swung off the ridge and were coming after him. That meant they had not reached the top, or seen Kiowa leading Rose and Hoffinger to safety. With only three men guarding him—and not doing a very good job of it—wily old Vern Hassle ought to escape, backed by Sandy and the Henry. Dusty knew that he could rely on the two corporals not to make their move too early.

Much as he would have liked to watch until Hassle escaped, Dusty faced the front and concentrated on the work at hand. The horse he rode had speed, endurance and was in the peak of condition. While making his arrangements, he had transferred every piece of equipment to the second of his relay, retaining only the clothes he wore and his gunbelt to add weight to his saddle. Being lighter than the majority of his pursuers, a superior rider to them all and far better mounted, he felt sure that he could eventually leave the Yankees behind.

However, he must not do so too quickly. First he had to lure them well clear of his companions. That would call for careful judgment, keeping close enough to encourage them to continue the chase, yet at a distance where they would be unlikely to hit him with their revolvers. Also he must try to nurse his horse so that it kept something in reserve in case of emergency.

From the cracking of shots that mingled with the drumming of hooves from behind him, Dusty concluded that some of the Yankees were trying to hit him. None of the bullets came close enough for him to be aware of their passing and he had no intention of returning the fire.

After covering about a mile, Dusty twisted cautiously around. Without disturbing his balance on the black's back, he studied his pursuers. Already the two sections had mixed together, which meant those from the rear party had driven their mounts extra-hard to catch up. The gap between Dusty and the leaders remained about the same, but the rest were beginning to string out. Poorer riders and weaker horses were already feeling the strain.

"Keep coming, you Yankee gentlemen!" Dusty gritted, turning forward. "The further you follow me, the better Mrs.—no, she said I could call her 'Rose'—the better her chances."

Koebel for one had no thought of calling off the pursuit. Raking with his spurs, he goaded his lathered mount to greater efforts. Anxiety gnawed at him as he passed among the sergeant's party. He hoped that none of the shots being fired would hit the Texan before he had assumed command once more. Avid for the prestige, and promotion, that would come from carrying out Trumpeter's unusual order, he gave no thought to the strain he was imposing upon his horse. Instead he forced it to stride out faster. Man after man fell behind him and at last he ranged himself alongside his sergeant. Glancing over his shoulder, the non-com stiffened as he recognized the officer.

"What's up?" the sergeant demanded, starting to rein in and wondering if they had fallen into a trap, with a large force of Texas Light Cavalry following to spring it on them.

"Keep going!" Koebel yelled back. "Get him. It's Dusty Fog!"

Which explained almost everything, particularly the officer's display of frenzied eagerness, to the experienced non-com. Trumpeter's order regarding Dusty Fog had aroused much speculation amongst the enlisted men. A long-serving soldier, the sergeant understood Koebel's motives. Equally aware of the benefits to be gained, the three-bar urged his horse on with renewed vigour.

Another mile was covered, without the distance between pursuers and pursued changing. No matter how the Yankees spurred their horses, the small Texan remained just as far ahead.

A vague suspicion began to creep over the sergeant and he remembered how he had once seen a fox run before a pack of hounds to lead them from its cubs. Maybe Dusty Fog was drawing the patrol away from something, or somebody, of importance. If so, he was succeeding. Looking back, the non-com saw that at least half of the patrol had already been forced to halt and the remainder straggled well behind.

"It's no use!" the sergeant shouted. "We'll kill the horses trying to catch up with him!"

From his mount's uneven gait, Koebel knew the man spoke the truth. Yet he refused to give up the attempt when the chance of promotion and acclaim rode less than a quarter of a mile ahead.

"Keep after him!" Koebel croaked, slamming his spurs brutally against the heaving flanks of his horse. "We'll get him ye—"

The stabbing of the spurs proved Koebel's undoing. Gamely trying to respond, the horse missed its footing, staggered and fell. Pitching over its head, the officer landed hard and skidded along the ground.

Taking warning from Koebel's fate, the sergeant brought his mount to a stop. Without a backwards glance, he dropped to the ground and snatched the Springfield carbine from the saddle-boot. Breathing hard, he sank on to his right knee. With his left elbow supppported on the raised knee, he still found the exertions of the gruelling ride prevented him from taking aim. Try as he might, he could not stop the barrel wavering in tune with the expansion and contraction of his struggling lungs. More in hope than expectancy, he squeezed the trigger at a moment when the sights lined on Dusty. It was a gesture of desperation. Clearly the bullet had no effect. Giving a resigned shrug, the sergeant stood up. Before he could reload, the small Texan would be out of range.

Other members of the patrol came up and reined in their lathered, leg-weary horses, watching Dusty continue to ride away. Booting his carbine, the sergeant went to Koebel's side. Bending, he examined the officer and decided that Koebel could count himself a lucky man. While his shoulder and arm had been broken by the fall, its result might easily have been fatal.

"Are we going after him, serge?" a soldier gasped.

"The hell we are!" the non-com replied; but did not mention that he now believed they should never have started the chase. "We'll rest the hosses, do what we can for the luff, then head back and see what's on the other side of that ridge. Only," he finished to himself, "by now we'll likely be way too late."

A point with which Dusty was in complete agreement as he twisted his torso and looked back. Satisfied that the patrol would not trouble him again, he allowed the black to slow down. Rose ought to be safe by now, so Dusty dismounted and gave thought to making good his own escape.

At about the same time that Dusty found himself free to make for the Ouachita River, Lieutenant Frost tiptoed nervously into his commanding general's presence. Seated at his desk, Trumpeter raised a haggard face and stared at his aide.

"The search of the town's finished, sir," Frost reported. "Nothing's been found. No word from the patrol we sent out towards the Arkadelphia section of the Ouachita."

"They won't do any good!" Trumpeter spat out. "You should have sent out more than one patrol."

While organizing the pursuit of Rose Greenhow and her rescuers had not been Frost's responsibility, he knew better than to raise the point. Brought back to the general's residence by the clamour of the alarm bell, Frost had found considerable reluctance amongst the rest of the staff to report Rose's escape to Trumpeter. It had fallen on Frost to break the news that the general's prize captive—whose arrest would divert attention from the unfortunate incidents of the lost remounts and Snake Ford—had been set free.

Frost had thought that Trumpeter would suffer a heart-seizure on reading Dusty Fog's entry in the Guard Report Book. Hurling the book at the wall, Trumpeter had cursed and raged like a madman, but had done nothing to take control of and correlate the hunt for the woman. Stripped of men for the assault on the Snake Ford, the garrison could not do a thorough job and hold the town against possible Rebel attack.

"I'd never have suspected Hoffinger—" Frost began, then realized that the comment had not been the most tactful he could have made.

"He's to be shot on sight!" Trumpeter snarled. "All of them are!"

"Yes, sir," Frost replied in a flat, neutral tone that still implied his doubt that the chance would arise.

Sinking his head on to his hands, Trumpeter ignored his aide. Thoughts churned and tumbled across the general's mind. All too clearly he could see the diabolical plot worked by the Rebels to discredit him. They were afraid to have a man of his superlative brilliance in a position of importance. While he had been tied to a desk in Washington, he was innocuous to their hated cause. Put in command of the Union's Army of Arkansas—last area of Confederate supremacy—his guiding genius would mean a turning point for the North. So the Rebel scum had conspired to bring about his removal.

Of course nobody had suspected Hoffinger. Getting him into Trumpeter's confidence had been almost clever.

Thinking back, the general recalled that it was Hoffinger's idea to collect the remounts in that unorthodox manner. He could also have learned of the forged order and been prepared to give the information to his companion-in-evil *Captain* Dusty Fog. If the two incidents did not prove sufficient to remove Trumpeter, they had arranged for the "denouncing" of the woman as Rose Grenhow. Then, after the general had reported her capture to Washington, conspired with members of the garrison to set her free.

They thought that they were smart, but they underestimated the man against whom they pitted their feeble wits. Soon, very soon, they would learn their mistake. Maybe not so soon in the case of Hoffinger and the woman. The Rebel Secret Service would move them to a place temporarily beyond his reach. Not so the other participant in the vile plot. Dusty Fog would remain in Arkansas; a living reminder pointing the finger of scorn at Trumpeter. Something must be done about that and Trumpeter knew what it was to be.

"Who can get in contact with the guerillas, Mr. Frost?" the general asked, raising his head.

"A few of the officers know members of different bands, sir," Frost answered.

"Get as many who can reach guerilla leaders as you can," Trumpeter ordered, picking up his pen and drawing a sheet of official paper towards him. "And do it quickly!"

CHAPTER FOURTEEN

Trumpeter'd Admire to See You Dead

"Believe me, Betty, Georgina, being a spy is a terrible life," Rose Greenhow told the two girls as they approached the big house which served as the combined headquarters of Ole Devil Hardin's staff and the Texas Light Cavalry. "Oh, I know it sounds romantic, gay and noble, but it isn't. You have to do things which sicken you; let men you despise paw and maul you to win their confidences, lie, cheat, steal—even kill. I've done all that and hated every minute of it."

Seven days had gone by since Rose's release from captivity. Her escape, after passing the 3rd Cavalry patrol, had been uneventful. Guided by the corporals and Kiowa, she had crossed the Ouachita and spent a worrying twenty-four hours until Dusty joined them. Changing into her own clothes, she had delivered her information to Ole Devil and now waited to return to the East. She had been made welcome and treated as a honoured guest by everybody, although there had been a certain hostility on the part of Company "C" until Dusty had returned unharmed.

Since their arrival, small, petite, black haired and beautiful Betty Hardin and slightly taller, buxom, blonde and pretty Georgina Blaze had devoted much of their time to trying to enlist, with Rose's aid, as spies. From the first, she had attempted to dissuade them from the idea and, with her departure imminent, increased her efforts. Looking at the eager young faces, she wondered if they took her words to heart. Betty appeared to be partially convinced, but Georgina seemed as determined as ever to join the Confederate States' Secret Service.

Situated on the edge of Prescott, the house had been built with its front away from the town. From its porch, one could look across the gardens to the rolling, wood-covered hills. The nearest slope rose about half a mile away, covered with bushes and trees that still offered feeding terrain for an occasional Kansas whitetail deer.

A black horse stood saddled and ground-hitched in front of the main entrance and Ole Devil Hardin strode from the house with Dusty Fog at his side. Seeing the woman and girls coming towards them, the general threw a frosty grin at his nephew.

"Good afternoon, General," Rose greeted.

"Mrs. Greenhow," Old Devil answered, directing a cold stare at the girls without it having any visible effect. "I hope these two young misses haven't been bothering you."

"On the contrary," Rose smiled. "I find them most refreshing and delightful. They remind me of when I was young."

"That's strange," Old Devil growled. "They have just the opposite effect on *me*. May we expect you at the ball tonight, Mrs. Greenhow?"

"You must come," Betty insisted, black eyes twinkling. "Why grand-papa gets quite lively when he throws away his walking-cane and takes the shawl from his tired old shoulders."

An explosive snort broke from Ole Devil, but a smile played on the corners of his lips. Possibly no other person would have dared to make such a comment.

The ball was to celebrate the successful conclusion of the Snake Ford affair. While strengthening the defences on the rim, Colonel Barnett had also been preparing for the inevitable time when the Union Army assembled such force that they would sweep the Confederate soldiers back by sheer weight of numbers. He had held on, defeating lesser attacks while cavalry patrols harassed the Yankees' flanks and rear, until receiving Wexler's warning of the massive reinforcements approaching. Then, in accordance with Ole Devil's orders, had made ready to withdraw.

After a night's artillery bombardment, Colonel Verncombe had launched an attack at strength in the grey light of dawn. Leading his men forward under heavy cannon fire from across the river, he had been puzzled by the lack of response from the Confederate positions ahead. Neither the captured Napoleons in their protective earthwork nor the figures in the trenches responded to the sight of the advancing enemy. Verncombe had soon learned why this was.

During the night, the Confederate defenders had fallen back to their own side of the river. They left behind dummies armed with useless, rusted rifles and wooden models of Napoleons for the Yankees to capture. Made at Barnett's instigation, the decoys had been moved in under the cover of darkness over four nights and were substituted without any report of it reaching Verncombe. Furious at having been tricked, the assault force continued its advance; only to be halted after heavy losses at the river's eastern edge. Seeing the impossibility of crossing the ford in the face of such heavy, concentrated and determined opposition, Verncombe wisely refrained from making the attempt.

So the Union's Army of Arkansas felt no pleasure at retaking the strip of territory. Maybe the Northern newspapers would enthuse over the success and probably regard it as the prelude to Trumpeter's promised advance into Texas, but the men concerned knew better. Once more they held the east side of the Snake Ford, but could go no farther; and taking it had cost many lives without the consolation of a corresponding number of Rebel dead. They were even denied the weak pleasure of retaking the captured Napoleon battery.

Ole Devil considered that there was cause for celebration. Making Barnett the guest-of-honour would be a public demonstration that the general did not blame him for accepting the forced order.

"I'll be honoured to attend, General," Rose said. "If you will promise me a dan—"

Two shots cracked from the slope in the background, one deep followed almost immediately by another lighter in pitch. Breaking off her request, Rose joined the others in looking for signs of who had fired.

"They came from up near the top, sir," Dusty said, pointing. "I can't see anything for the bushes."

"It could be somebody from the regiment out hunting," Georgina suggested.

"Could be," Dusty admitted dubiously. "The first sounded like a heavy rifle, but the other was a Henry."

"I loaned Kiowa *your* Henry, Dusty," Betty put in. "He's promised to fetch a couple of tom-turkeys in. That could have been him."

"It could," Dusty agreed. "I reckon I'll ride up there and take a look."

"Do that, Dustine," Ole Devil confirmed. "Its probably nothing, but we may as well be sure."

Suspicious by nature and upbringing, Kiowa Cotton never entirely relaxed his vigilance. Even while returning from a successful turkey hunt, so close to his regiment's camp, he remained alert for any unusual sounds or sights. Coming across the fresh tracks of a single horse, he gave them a close scrutiny. Made about an hour before, they followed a route which struck him as curious and significant. Whoever rode the horse had taken pains to select an inconspicuous route. While a clear trail lay close by and could be seen from different points, the rider had kept clear of it.

Of course he might be one of Wexler's men delivering a report and wishing to keep his identity a secret. Or he could be a Yankee soldier on a scouting mission. Whatever his motive, Kiowa figured that the man rated investigation.

Dropping the bodies of two turkeys to the ground, the sergeant rode forward. Indian-bred, the horse he sat moved with an almost wild-animal silence. Kiowa knew the country around Prescott well enough to pin-point his exact location. If the mysterious rider continued in a straight line, he would arrive on the slope over-looking the headquarters building.

A slight movement from ahead brought Kiowa to an immediate halt. For a moment he could see nothing out of the ordinary. Then another movement drew his attention to it. Slowly the shape of a horse, standing amongst the bushes some distance away, came into focus. Only a flicker of an ear had betrayed it, for its dun coat merged well with the shadows. Without its involuntary movement, Kiowa might have ridden closer and alarmed it.

Dropping from his saddle, Kiowa slipped the Henry from its boot. He left his horse ground-hitched and darted forward on foot. Making use of every bit of cover, he moved in an arc that ought to keep him from disturbing the dun. Silently he climbed up the ridge, slipping through the head-high clumps of buffalo-berry bushes until he passed over the top. Then he caught his first glimpse of the horse's owner.

One glance told Kiowa that, whatever he might be, the man had no innocent purpose. Big, gaunt, with a wide-brimmed hat, clad in fringed buckskins with pants tucked into unpolished riding boots, he lowered a small telescope through which he had been studying the front of the distant house. Coming to his feet, a powder-horn suspended from his left shoulder, he thrust the telescope into his waist-band. Then he picked up the long Sharps 1859 rifle and advanced like a hunter stalking his prey.

Unless Kiowa missed his guess, the prey stood outside the big house. Even at that distance, the sergeant could make out the shapes on the proch. With the aid of his telescope, the man would have identified them.

Working with Dusty Fog had taught Kiowa to think before acting. If the man intended to kill somebody at the house, discovering who and why was mighty important. So Kiowa neither spoke nor fired at the intruder. Instead he moved forward, meaning to take a living, talking prisoner if he could. Before he had taken three steps, he felt the breeze, up to then blowing directly into his face, veer to the left. It would be carrying his scent to the man's waiting horse. An animal so well trained would have learned other lessons than merely standing like a statue. Sure enough, even as Kiowa realized the danger, the horse cut loose with a loud snort.

Instantly the man whirled around. Seeing Kiowa, he continued raising his rifle which was already swinging to-

wards his shoulder. He moved fast. Far too swiftly for the
sergeant to dare take chances. With the Sharps lifting to
point at him, Kiowa flung himself sideways. Accurate as it
might be at long ranges, the Sharp's length and weight
made it clumsy and awkward to manoeuvre at speed.
Going down in a rolling dive, Kiowa snapped the Henry
into line and fired. His shot came as an echo of the Sharp's
deep boom. Lead screamed over the sergeant's head in tes-
timony to the nearness of his escape. His own bullet tore
into the man's chest, ploughing up to burst out at the back.

Throwing the Henry's lever down and up, Kiowa saw
the man turn, hunch forward, drop the Sharps and fall. The
sergeant rose, advancing cautiously with the repeater ready
to speak at the first hostile move. Extending his left foot,
he rolled the man over. For a moment the other's eyes
glowed hate, then they glazed and the gaunt body went
limp.

"Now who the hell are you?" Kiowa mused. "And
what'd you come to do?"

A question which Dusty repeated almost word for word
on his arrival.

"What do you reckon, Kiowa?" he went on, looking at
the body.

"He was watching the house through that telescope,
then started to move in for a shot at one of you who was
outside."

"Nobody would want Cousin Betty or Cousin Georgie
dead," Dusty said. "Which means he was after Uncle Devil
or Mrs. Rose."

"You was there, 'long with the others," Kiowa pointed
out. "And Trumpeter'd admire to see you dead."

"Hell, I'm not that important so's he'd send a sharp-
shooter special to get me," Dusty protested. "Mrs. Rose,
maybe. Or even Uncle Devil, but not me."

"He was after one of you, that's all I know," Kiowa
drawled. "I've been through his pockets, ain't nothing in
'em to say who he is."

"Back-track him, see where he's come from," Dusty

ordered. "I'll have him and his horse taken in. Maybe Mrs. Rose can help out when she sees him."

On learning of the reason for the shooting, Rose expressed her interest and suggested that she should supervise the search. Waving aside her apologies for interfering, Dusty admitted that it had been his intention to ask her do so. Accompanying the small Texan to the barn farthest from the house, she set to work. Drawing aside the blanket which covered the man, she looked at his face.

"I don't know him, but I don't pretend to know every member of the Yankee Secret Service," she said. "You've had him stripped, that's good. While I start on his clothes, check under his arms, between his legs, in the cheeks of his arse and among his hair. You can discount him having anything in his ears or mouth, or up his nose, he wouldn't carry documents concealed there for any length of time." She made a wry face and went on, "Maybe I should have had Betty and Georgie come help me. Then they'd really know what a spy has to do."

"If you'd rather, I'll do the searching," Dusty offered.

"No," Rose answered. "This's work I've been trained to do."

From what Dusty saw, after following her instructions about searching the corpse, Rose had learned her lessons well. No detail was too small for her to examine. First she crushed every article of clothing between her fingers, held close to her ear so that any faint crackle of concealed paper could be detected, then checked the thickness of the cloth in case another piece of material bearing identification was stitched between the layers. The hat was studied inside and out, the sole, heel and upper of each boot ripped apart, the waist and gunbelt torn to pieces. Brought along at Rose's request, the armourer stripped the man's weapons to bare essentials and the saddler gave the horse's leatherwork an equally thorough going over. Even the telescope was dismantled to be scrutinized. The dun horse received as careful a search as had been given to its master.

"Nothing," Rose announced, after the powder horn had been emptied and split open to expose its interior. "I'll stake my life that 'he's carrying nothing to identify him—And yet I've never known a Yankee agent not to."

"If he'd've had anything, you'd've found it," Dusty praised, coming over from where he had been washing his hands and arms after the messy business of examining the horse. "Could he be a U.S. Army sharp-shooter sent to kill you?"

"It's possible," Rose admitted, showing her pleasure at the compliment "From what Kiowa told you, the man had been watching the house for some time."

"That's what he said and he can read tracks real good. The feller watched the house until you met us outside, then moved forward to start shooting. Which means he was after one of us. If he'd just wanted to kill at random, he wouldn't't've waited. There were fellers moving about all the time. I figure he was after you, or Uncle Devil."

"Some of the Yankee Secret Service would like to see me dead, I admit. But it's not likely they'd go at it that way. Killing Devil would throw your Army into confusion, perhaps. Not for long, but long enough to let the Yankees launch an offensive before he could be replaced. Except that 'Oakland' would have warned us if a move of that magnitude was planned. It couldn't be kept a secret."

"Not from Wex—Oakland, anyways," Dusty agreed.

"There's another alternative, Dusty," Rose said. "Trumpeter could have sent the man after you."

"Kiowa reckoned that," the small Texan replied, "Hell, he couldn't want revenge bad enough to risk a sharp-shooter* just to get it. Even if the feller was a sharp-shooter that is."

"He wasn't on that slope just to admire the scenery," Rose objected.

"Do you reckon he's Army?"

"There you've got me, Dusty. That buckskin shirt, his trousers and gunbelt could have been bought anywhere west of the Mississippi. The boots are cavalry issue, so is his undershirt, which doesn't mean much as they can be bought easily enough. The hat could have been picked up

*Sharp-shooter: Civil war name for a sniper.

north or south of the Mason-Dixon line and is old enough to have been bought before the War. It doesn't help us."

"That's a Rocky Mountain saddle and the horse's range-bred," Dusty went on. "It's not carrying a brand of any kind."

"Neither his rifle nor revolver have U.S. Army proof-marks," Rose told him.

"Sharp-shooters mostly buy their own rifles," Dusty replied. "And a whole mess of fellers, especially from out West, fetched their revolvers along when they joined the army."

"It's puzzling," Rose sighed, thinking of one solution to the mystery but dismissing it as unworthy of serious consideration. "So we can only wait and see if Kiowa learns anything."

"That's about all," Dusty agreed, reaching much the same conclusion as Rose had and not mentioning it for similar reasons. "Anyways, I don't reckon there'll be another try until whoever sent him learns he didn't make it. Sharp-shooters aren't so plentiful or easy come-by that they'd chance losing more than one at a go."

"Talking of going," Rose gasped as she glanced through the open door of the barn. "It's long gone time we went and dressed for the ball."

Turning, Dusty let out a low whistle of surprise. He had not realized how long the search had taken. Night had fallen and already the big house was glowing with lights, while the activity about the place warned that the festivities would soon commence. So he told their assistants to clear up the barn, allowing Rose and himself to go to change their clothing. Rose had been fitted out with dresses on her arrival and had even managed to find a gown suitable for the occasion.

For Dusty's part, he knew that the casual, comfortable uniform worn on patrol would not meet with official approval that night. Reluctantly he made his way to the quarters he shared with Red, meaning to don the correct full dress. On his arrival, he found his striker waiting. Dick Cody had spent most of his adult life attending to Army

officers' welfare. While proud of his current charge, he did
not approve of the way Dusty ignored the *Manual of Dress
Regulations*. Nothing pleased Cody more than to watch his
officer going forth in a double-breasted, skirted tunic, em-
bellished with a black silk cravat, white gloves, trousers
instead of riding breeches, correct accoutrements and
sabre.

"I'm sure pleasured that you changed your mind, sir,"
Cody greeted.

"How's that?" Dusty asked.

"About attending the ball in your dress uniform."

"What else would I wear tonight?"

"But Miss Georgina came and said you'd decided to go
in your skirtless tunic and riding breeches, sir," the old
striker explained, looking bewildered.

"She must've been joshing you," Dusty replied. His
cousin knew of Cody's feelings about the matter of uniform
and was not averse to a joke.

"Joshing or not, sir," Cody answered indignantly, "She
took them with her. And your hat, boots and gunbelt."

"Gunbelt!" Dusty snapped. "Damn it, Cousin Georgie's
gone way too far this time. I'll pound some sense into her
fool hide, see if I don't."

"Yes, sir," Cody agreed enthusiastically. "She sounded
so sincere that I didn't doubt that you had sent her."

"I hope she sounds that way when I get through with
her," Dusty growled. "What damned fool game is she
playing?"

Before Cody could express an opinion, they heard a
disturbance from the town. Somebody shouted a warning
which mingled with a revolver shot. Then another shot
craked, followed by more shouting; this time from several
places.

"It coming from Main street, sir!" Cody stated.

"Sounds like it," Dusty agreed. "I'd best go and see
what's happening."

CHAPTER FIFTEEN

I'll Kill Him Where He Stands

"It's working, Cousin Betty!" Georgina Blaze enthused as she strode along the centre of Main Street dressed in Dusty's uniform, hat, boots and gunbelt. "We're taking them all in."

"Out here in the street, maybe," Betty answered. "It won't be so easy in good light. You know, Cousin Dusty's not going to like you walking around in his uniform."

Smaller than Georgina, Betty had borrowed clothes from one of the drummer-boys. In the hope of making her disguise more acceptable, she carried his drum on her back. Gripping its V-shaped sling in her left hand, she looked along the almost deserted street. Lights showed in a number of buildings, from many of which came the sounds of people enjoying themselves. Ahead was the Shenandoah Hotel, its porch and hitching rail deserted despite the noisy evidence of revelry from within.

"Why he won't mind me borrowing his old uniform," Georgina protested, trying to sound more confident than she felt. "Will he?"

"He'll not be pleased," Betty guessed. "I surely hope Tommy hasn't shown him that *yoko-guruma* throw he taught me."

"That—?"

"*Yoko-guruma,*" Betty repeated. "It means lateral wheel or something and it's a dilly."

"It sure sounds that way," Georgina smiled. "And if we can walk the length of Main Street, then get by the guards to the ball dressed like this, it will show Rose we're smart enough to be spies."

"Or convince her more than ever that we're not," Betty replied. "It's a *loco* trick—and before you get into a tizz, I agreed to try it."

A man came from an alley opposite to the hotel, slouching towards the girls. Medium-sized, stocky, he wore civilian clothes of sober colours and kept his right hand behind his back. At the same moment, the door of the Shenandoah's barroom opened and Hoffinger stepped on to the porch. Halting, the chubby dude looked in each direction along the street. Seeing the man approaching the two uniformed figures, he stiffened slightly. For a moment he studied the girls, then his eyes went to something about the man which could not be visible to them.

"Air you Cap'n Dusty Fog?" asked the man from the alley.

"I am," Georgina agreed, making her voice sound husky.

"Look out!" Hoffinger screamed, leaping forward.

The warning came too late. Hearing Georgina answer in the affirmative, the man brought his hand into view. Shock momentarily numbed the girls, causing them to ignore Hoffinger's warning; for they saw the hand held a long-barrelled Army Colt that lifted to line at Georgina. Muzzle-blast flared redly on the night-darkened street as a .44 bullet spun from the revolver to drive into the blonde's left breast. Cocking back the hammer swiftly, the man started to swing the barrel towards Betty. Then he heard the thud of Hoffinger's feet and turned to meet what might prove a greater danger than the diminutive "drummer-boy."

Anger filled Hoffinger, wiping away his love of peace. Recklessly he plunged from the sidewalk, striding determinedly toward the man. He gave no thought to the consequences of his actions, or his inadequacy to deal with an armed man. Since his arrival in Prescott, he had convinced his abductors of his pacific intentions and complete lack of desire to escape. So they allowed him to roam around unattended and his jovial nature had won him many friends. Popular he might be in all walks of the town's society, but not sufficiently trusted to be allowed to carry a gun. Being unarmed did not prevent him going forward.

Coming around fast, the man slanted his Colt in Hoffinger's direction. Aware that he could not reach the other in time to prevent him shooting, the little dude hoped that he might buy the second girl—whom he recognized despite her disguise—the opportunity to run to safety.

Only Betty did not run. Born of a fighting stock, spirited and self-reliant in her own right, she recovered rapidly from the shock of the attack. More than that, she saw Hoffinger's peril and knew that he would die unless something was done in a hurry. Flashing up her hands, she gripped the drum with the intention of ridding herself of it to be free to help her rescuer. Even as she raised it over her head, she saw a better use for it than hurling it aside. Swinging it high, she took a stride towards Georgina's assailant.

With death staring him in the face, Hoffinger saw something rise into the air behind the man. Then, accompanied by a dull boom, the other's head disappeared inside Betty's drum. Again the Colt roared, but surprise had caused its barrel to be deflected and its bullet tore a furrow through the hotel's name-board instead of into the dude's chubby frame.

Ducking his head, Hoffinger butted into the man as he tried to remove the drum. At the same moment, Betty smashed her interlaced-fingered hands into his kidney region from behind. The impact bore the man backwards, despite Betty's blow, and he went down with Hoffinger on top of him. Mouthing curses, the little dude flailed inexpertly at his victim. On the street, doors were flung open as people appeared to investigate the disturbance. Bursting out of the hotel's barroom, Billy Jack and other members of Company "C" swarmed forward. Still striking out wildly, Hoffinger felt himself gripped and dragged upright.

"Ease off, Ossie!" Billy Jack growled, clinging to the dude's right arm. "We'll tend to him."

Slowly Hoffinger's fighting rage died away. Looking around, he saw the man firmly held by Sergeant Weather and Sandy McGraw. Then the dude's eyes turned to where Betty knelt at her cousin's side.

"Oh Lord!" the black-haired girl was sobbing. "What have we done? What *have* we done?"

Everything was in confusion as people milled around and asked questions, or stared in bewilderment at what they saw. Billy Jack's lackadaisical pose left him and for once he showed why he held the rank of sergeant major in the Texas Light Cavalry's elite Company "C."

"Quiet it down!" he roared. Then, as silence fell, he turned to Hoffinger and spoke in a gentler tone. "What happened?"

"I—I don't know," the dude admitted, struggling to think and quieten his churned-up emotions. "The—I saw —the young ladies—knew she wasn't Captain Fog—saw his gun—I shouted, but it was too late."

Which left a lot unexplained, but helped Billy Jack to understand a little of what had happened. He knew Georgina to be a practical joker, which might account for why she was wearing Cap'n Dusty's clothes. Seeing her lying there had given the sergeant major a hell of a shock. Now he realized that her disguise had, for some reason, brought tragic results.

The crowd opened up to let Dusty come through. Striding forward, expecting to find there had been a quarrel ending in gun-play between the participants, he slammed to a halt. For a moment he could hardly credit the message of his eyes. Then he moved forward, dropping to one knee at Betty's side. One glance at Georgina told him that she was beyond help. Blood still spread slowly on the left breast of the borrowed tunic, but he had seen enough of wounds to know that she was dead.

"What happened?" Dusty asked and the listeners could hardly recognize his voice.

Twisting around, Betty flung herself into Dusty's arms and sobbed a reply;

"He—that man—asked Georgie—'Are you Cap'n Dusty Fog?'—and when—when she said she was—she— he—he shot her."

An ugly, menacing rumble rose from the crowd, directed at the man held by the non-coms. It died away as Dusty glared around. Then the small Texan looked at the prisoner and sucked in a deep breath.

"He asked Georgie if she was me," Dusty said quietly, "and shot her when she said she was."

"Y-Yes," Betty gulped, shocked by his tone into momentarily forgetting her horror and grief.

"Then it looks like he got the wrong one."

Saying that, Dusty gently freed himself from Betty's arms. Just as gently, he removed the gunbelt from Georgina's body. In a silence that could almost be felt, he strapped on the belt and fastened the tips of the holsters to his thighs. Moving clear of the girls, he addressed his men.

"Turn him loose and put a gun in his hand!"

"Cap'n—!" Billy Jack put in and he did not intend to continue with one of his usual unmeant doleful warnings or complaints.

"Do it!" Dusty snapped. "Or I'll kill him where he stands!"

Billy Jack nodded to Sandy and Weather. As they released the man, the sergeant major took out his right hand Colt. Sobbing for breath, the man fell back against the hotel's hitching rail. Slowly Billy Jack walked forward and thrust his Colt into the man's right hand, then stepped aside.

"All right, *hombre,*' Dusty said. "You want to kill Dusty Fog. Well, I'm him. Get to doing it."

Almost recovered from the effects of the combined attack, the man stared numbly at the *big* Texan. Everything about Dusty filled the man, hard as he was, with a gnawing terror. Cold merciless retribution as certain as the hangman's noose showed on the young face. The powerful figure stood poised like a cougar waiting to spring, hands held out from its sides with fingers slightly crooked ready to close about the white handles of the holstered Colts. That was no man he faced, but a machine, a deadly highly-developed machine with just one purpose—to kill him.

"N-No!" the man croaked, finding himself unable to throw the gun away.

"Count to three, Billy Jack," Dusty ordered—and it was an order, despite the cat's purr gentle way he spoke. "By three, he'll use that gun or die."

"One!" Billy Jack said, for he could no more resist than the ashen-faced killer could toss aside the Colt. The rest of the crowd stood as if turned to stone, oblivious of the people who came from the big house, conscious only of the scene before them.

"Two!" Billy Jack counted.

"No!" a woman's voice shouted. "Dusty. No!"

Face pallid and raging with emotion, Rose Greenhow ran along the street ahead of the party from the ball. She had heard from a Negro maid of the girl's idea to impress her and planned to surprise the would-be spies on their arrival. Waiting with members of the guard to capture them, she had heard the shooting. On learning from where it originated, Rose had an almost clairvoyant idea of what had happened. Sending a man to notify Ole Devil of the trouble, she set off to look into it and prayed she might be wrong. All too soon she knew how right she had been. No humane considerations motivated her call to Dusty. The man cowering against the hitching rail could answer questions—but only if he stayed alive.

"Three!" Billy Jack said.

"Captain Fog!" Rose screamed in the same breath.

At the sergeant major's word, Dusty's right hand moved. All the long, hard hours of practising his draw, backed by the carefully considered design and excellent workmanship of his gunbelt, permitted him to fetch out the long barrelled Colt with blinding speed. He had never moved faster than at that moment. Out came the revolver, its hammer drawn back by his thumb and trigger going to the rear under the pressure of his forefinger as the seven-and-a-half inch "civilian pattern" barrel* turned towards its target. Straight as if pulled by a magnetic force, Dusty's Colt lined at the man's head.

---

*The normal Army model had an eight inch barrel.

And did not fire!

With the trigger depressed to the full and thumb quivering on the verge of freeing the hammer, reason returned to the small Texan. A concerted gasp rolled from the spectators. Letting out a moan, the man dropped Billy Jack's revolver and turned to sob into his arms against the hitching rail.

"Clear the street, all of you who aren't involved!" Dusty ordered, lowering the hammer and returning the Colt to its holster.

Like snow before a fire, the crowd melted away. There were at least two officers senior in rank to Dusty present, but they withdrew like the rest. By the time Billy Jack had retrieved his Colt and the man's revolver, only the people directly concerned with the incident remained. Ole Devil arrived fast, accompanied by Colonel Mannen Blaze, Dusty's father and others of the family.

"What's happened, Dustine?" the general demanded while the women moved towards Betty and the body.

Slowly, fighting down her grief, Betty rose and faced the men to repeat in more detail the story she had told to Dusty. At its end, the Texan senior officers turned to Hoffinger.

"My thanks, sir," Ole Devil said.

"I—I was too late," the dude mumbled, seeming to have shrunk into himself and showing none of his usual urbane poise.

"You saved Cousin Betty's life," Dusty put in. "With your permission, Uncle Devil, I aim to let Trumpeter know that Mr. Hoffinger's not a traitor—"

"Trumpeter!" croaked the killer, turning from the hitching rail and drawing every eye his way. "It was Trumpeter who offered the reward to any man who could kill you, Cap'n Fog."

"What was that?" Ole Devil barked, striding forward.

Rose and Dusty beat the general to the man and the small Texan said, "Tell it fast and all!"

"It's true!" the man croaked, reaching inside his jacket. "I've got the letter he sent to—!"

"Let him take it out!" Ole Devil ordered as Sandy and Weather sprang on to the man and grabbed his arms. Taking the folded sheet of paper which the killer produced, he read it. "Well I'll be damned!"

"Look at it, Hondo!" Colonel Blaze said, after receiving and studying the paper. "It's damnable."

Looking like a taller, older version of Dusty, Major Hondo Fog read the message. Without comment, he handed it to Rose.

"To whom it may concern," Rose read aloud. "I, Horace Trumpeter, General Commanding the United States' Army of Arkansas, will pay the sum of one thousand dollars with no questions asked, to any man who produces proof that he has killed the rebel and traitor who calls himself Captain Dusty Fog." She paused, then continued, "It's signed by him and marked with his official seal. Who are you?"

"Ike Smith," the man, to whom the question had been directed, answered. "I was one of Toby Mattison's boys—"

"A lousy border-jumper!" Billy Jack ejaculated.

"Who else knows about this letter?" Rose demanded, ignoring the comment.

"Nobody's far's I know. I saw Toby get it and when he didn't tell us what it was I snuck it from him."

"Is there a big, gaunt Westerner in your gang?" Rose asked. "He wears a large grey hat, buckskin shirt and trousers, cavalry boots. Rides a dun gelding and uses a Sharps rifle."

"Sounds like the feller in Stegner's bunch, the one they call Rocky Mountains," Smith answered. "He allows to be a better'n fair shot with that rifle."

"And *that's* why we didn't find any identification!" Rose said. "He was a guerilla trying to collect the bounty."

"I wondered if he might be one," Dusty confessed. "Only I knew no lousy guerilla'd come after any of us just to serve the North."

"The same thing occurred to me," Rose admitted. "But it seemed so unlikely—Why didn't I speak. We could have been on guard—"

"You weren't to know," Ole Devil told her gently. "None of us could imagine a general of the United States Army would stoop to doing it."

"I *should* have realized!" Rose insisted. "All along I've known Trumpeter was a rabid radical, the kind who'd break if he found himself under any strain. I ought to have guessed it was possible he'd hire men to kill Dusty."

"Nobody blames you, Rose," Hondo declared; then his face clouded. Before the War, he had fast been gaining a name as one of the most shrewd peace officers in Texas. During that time he had developed the habit of looking at any incident from all its angles. Doing the same on the Prescott street, he reached an ugly conclusion. "If Trumpeter sent those bounty notes to Mattison and Stegner, he'll have passed them to the other guerilla bands."

"And it's likely that they'll be trying to claim the reward," Rose went on.

"That's how I see it," Dusty remarked in the same quiet voice with which he had ordered Billy Jack to arm Smith.

"It'll have to be stopped!" Rose stated. "Grant wouldn't allow it if he heard of Trumpeter's actions."

"Grant's a long ways off," Dusty pointed out. "Time we can get word to him, could be somebody else'll have been killed in mistake for me. No ma'am, Rose. There's only one man who can stop that bounty quick enough to do any good. The feller who's offering it."

"*Trumpeter!*" Rose gasped, staring at the small Texan as she began to understand what he meant.

"Yes'm. And I'm fixing to give him a chance to earn his own bounty."

"He'd never cancel the offer!" Ole Devil said, then realization struck him. "You mean that you're going to face him down?"

"Yes, sir," Dusty confirmed.

"Not alone you won't!" Red Blaze declared. He had arrived with the others and listened to the conversation while comforting Georgina's mother. "The whole Company, the whole *regiment* comes to that. 'll be with you."

"They won't," Dusty contradicted. "Just me and four men're going."

"Who're the other *three?*" Red wanted to know.

"Billy Jack, Kiowa happen he's back in time, Vern Hassle—"

"I'll volunteer, Capn' Dusty," Sandy McGraw announced, beating Sergeant Weather to it by a split second.

"You, Sandy," Dusty confirmed. "This's no chore for a married man, Stormy. You'll run the Company as acting sergeant major while we're gone."

"Dusty, you can't—!" Rose protested.

"Those bounty letters won't be done with until one of us is dead," Dusty replied. "Already one innocent girl's been killed because of them. There could be others. So I'm going to stop them."

"What're we going to need, Cap'n Dusty?" asked Billy Jack.

And then the sergeant major, Red and Sandy realized that permission for the mission to proceed had not been given. So they turned their eyes towards Ole Devil. As always, he thought first but came to a decision without a waste of time.

"You think you can achieve something, Dustine?"

"I'm going to try," Dusty stated. "I won't take chances, sir. I want to get to Trumpeter too bad for that."

"What do you think, Hondo?" asked the general. "He's your son."

"And he's set on going," Hondo replied. "There's no way, short of hog-tying him, that'll stop him. And I know that, whatever he does, it'll be thought out carefully, not rushed at blind."

Which agreed with Ole Devil's summation. He had already made up his mind, but had needed the extra seconds to steel himself for giving the permission that might send two of his nephews and three good soldiers to their death. The fact that they would go with or without authority provided him with some small consolation; and he knew that something must be done to stop the guerillas acting on the bounty offer.

"Good luck, Dustine," he said. "If there's anything you need, ask for it."

"Let me go with you, Dusty," Betty put in. "Please. Lord! I could have talked Cousin Georgie out of this foolishness, but I didn't try. I'll go mad if I don't do something."

Looking at Betty, Rose felt that she must speak. This was no naive girl filled with ideas of how glamorous a life she might have as a spy. Betty had matured, grown up, changed in the minutes since Georgina had died. While aware of how dangerous the mission would be, Rose felt that Betty deserved a place on it and might be of assistance.

"Take her, Dusty," Rose begged. "I'd come with you, but I don't ride well enough and would slow you down."

Betty and Dusty faced each other, standing without speaking for several seconds. He knew that she would accept his refusal, but that things would never be the same between them again. So he nodded his head and said, "You can come."

CHAPTER SIXTEEN

General Trumpeter, Meet Captain Dusty Fog

Patrolling outside the eastern wall of General Trumpeter's residence was not a duty Private Sloan regarded with enthusiasm. Unlike on the other three sides, no gates pierced his part of the wall. So he could not stop and chat with the stationary sentries. The duty would have seemed less onerous if there had been any logical point on keeping watch that side. In addition to the ten-foot stone wall around the property, the nearest dwellings—a pair of smaller houses some fifty yards away—had been commandeered and were occupied with Union personnel. Anyways, who the hell among the Rebs would figure on sneaking in and killing old "Bugle-horn" Trumpeter. Fact being, from the hash he had made of things since his arrival, the Confederate States Army ought to be real keen to leave him in command.

Just about the only consolation Sloan could find came from his clothes. No longer did Zouave regiments wear fancy copies of frog-eating French uniforms, but dressed like honest-to-God American soldiers. He preferred even a forage cap to the Zouave fez. Over his infantry uniform, he wore an overcoat with a shorter cloak than that sported by cavalrymen. Around the coat was his well-polished cartridge-box belt, with leather sling, passing diagonally from the cartridge box on his right hip to the left shoulder, cap box, bayonet scabbard and canteen; although Sloan could not see the point of carrying the latter.

The sound of footsteps drew his attention to the gap between the adjacent houses. Bringing his rifle and bayonet to the required position—in case it was the officer-of-

the-day making rounds, rather than expecting to need the
weapons—he gave the prescribed challenge.

"Halt. Who goes there?"

"Now you-all don't think lil ole me's a Johnny Reb soldier, do you?" answered a feminine voice.

Peering through the darkness, Sloan made out the figure
of a girl coming towards him. Small, dainty, wearing a
sleeveless white blouse and a skirt of glossy black material,
she walked with an attractive hip-sway. Lowering his rifle,
Sloan grinned. Every enlisted man knew that the officers
entertained ladies—a *very* loose definition—in their
quarters, regardless of Regulations. So he saw nothing suspicious about her presence.

"Where you going, gal?" Sloan demanded, figuring he
had best not ask where she had been.

"Home," she replied. "Don't you-all tell me it's not allowed."

"It's after curfew," Sloan pointed out. "I'm supposed to
holler for the sergeant of the guard."

"If you do, he'll only take me off someplace and—
scold me a lil," the girl purred. "Now a big, strong, handsome gentleman like you won't let that happen to me, will
you?"

"What do *I* get if I don't?"

"A kiss—for starters."

Figuring that he could take the chance, even if no more
than a kiss came out of it, Sloan leaned his rifle against the
wall. Then he took a stride forward and put his arms
around the girl's waist. From what he felt, she wore nothing under the blouse. She was warm, inviting, yielding to
the force of his charm. As he lowered his face, she brought
up her hands to his shoulders. Savouring in anticipation the
coming kiss, he became aware that three men in uniform
were approaching from the gap through which the girl had
appeared. They were cavalry soldiers, going by their uniforms, but no *Union* cavalry wore gunbelts of that kind.

Even as Sloan's grip slackened, the girl slipped her right
leg between his spread apart feet. At the same time, she
thrust up her hands. The base of her palms rammed with

some force under his chin. Bright lights blazed briefly before Sloan's eyes. Deftly the girl hooked her advanced leg behind his left foot as the force of the double blow caused him to retreat. Tripping, he fell backwards and his skull smashed into the wall as he went down.

"Nice going, Cousin Betty!" Dusty Fog complimented, as he, Kiowa and Billy Jack sprang forward.

"Is he dead?" Betty Hardin inquired worriedly, watching the gangling sergeant major kneel by the sentry's motionless body.

All too clearly Betty saw what Rose Greenhow had meant about the unpleasant nature of a spy's work. There had been nothing gay, romantic, or noble in tricking the sentry, necessary though it might have been.

When Kiowa had returned, saying he had back-tracked the dead guerilla for five miles without learning anything, Dusty's party made ready to travel. With Betty wearing boy's clothing and all non-essentials left behind, they had made a fast but uneventful ride from Prescott.

Leaving Red and Sandy to guard the horses and, when the time came, cut the telegraph wires, Dusty took Betty and his men into Little Rock. Visiting Wexler, Dusty found him preparing to send a warning about Trumpeter's bounty offer. On learning of the events in Prescott, he put all his knowledge at Dusty's disposal. Not only had he made a very accurate map of the general's residence, but he gave a complete description of its staff and the manner in which it was guarded. With that done, he had continued to tell of the most recent developments.

Since Rose Greenhow's escape and learning—through rumours started by Wexler—of Hoffinger's "treachery," Trumpeter had become suspicious and uncommunicative; which explained the undertaker's delay in discovering the offer had been made. Not even the officers who had delivered the notes knew of the contents. On learning of the general's actions and obtaining one of the letters, Wexler had arranged for it to reach Colonel Verncombe. Little love was lost between the Dragoon and Trumpeter. Knowing Verncombe to be the most senior officer under the general,

Wexler had hoped that something might come of the colonel learning such an offer had been made.

Disinclined to wait in the hope that something *might* happen, Dusty had decided to go on with his plan. From what he had learned, he considered the eastern wall offered the best point of entry— if its sentry could be removed in silence. Rather than chance stalking the man across the open ground, he had arranged for Betty to act as a decoy. Warned of what she might need by Rose Greenhow, Betty had brought along suitable clothing. Consisting only of the blouse and skirt, borrowed from a girl who knew Billy Jack very well, the weight of her disguise had been negligible and proved its worth. Picking a time shortly after the sentries had been changed, she had done all Dusty required. The way she had handled Sloan was her own idea, backed with the training received from Tommy Okasi.

"He'll live," Billy Jack answered, unbuckling Sloan's cartridge belt.

"You're nearest his size," Dusty told the sergeant major. "Get dressed *pronto* and start walking his beat."

"I allus knowed you aimed to bust me," Billy Jack complained as he drew the cartridge-box's sling over the sentry's head. "Only I never figured it'd be to private in the *Yankee* Army."

"And a puddle-splasher at that," Betty went on, smiling weakly. "Why I'm shamed by your meanness, Cousin Dusty."

Glancing at his cousin, Dusty grinned. Often he had seen new recruits on their first dangerous mission relax and gain confidence from Billy Jack's gloomy wailing. Betty appeared to have thrown off her worry and concern, caused by the way she had deceived the sentry.

While Dusty kept watch, Billy Jack removed Sloan's accoutrements and overcoat. He donned the garments himself, leaving Betty and Kiowa to rope and gag the unconscious sentry.

"How'll I do?" Billy Jack inquired, putting on the Yankee's kepi.

"You'll get by, happen you keep your boots out of sight," Dusty replied.

Yankee infantry wore trousers and Jefferson bootees, but the overcoat was too short to hide the discrepancy.

"You could walk kind of scrunched up," Betty suggested.

"If that'd've been Cap'n Dusty," moaned the sergeant major, "He'd've told me to cut a foot or so off my legs."

"I *had* thought of that," Betty assured him, "but it would take too long."

"Let's go!" Dusty ordered. "You all know what to do. If I'm not back to you three minutes after any shooting starts, I'll be dead, so get away."

"Yo!" Kiowa answered, with as near emotion as he ever showed, moving to stand with his back to the wall.

Dusty placed his right foot in the sergeant's cupped hands and thrust upwards with his left leg. Assisted by Kiowa's lift, he rose and swung himself on to the garden wall. Lowering himself on the other side, he dropped into the garden. There he crouched against the wall, searching for signs that his arrival had been detected. Wexler had claimed that no sentries patrolled inside the grounds, but precautions cost nothing and kept a man alive. Certain at last that he was undetected, he began to move across the garden.

Passing amongst the bushes, Dusty pictured what his companions would be doing. Beyond the wall, Betty and Kiowa were dragging the sentry away while Billy Jack walked the beat. Then the girl would return, ready to stand and talk with the sergeant major if the north or south wall sentry happened to look. Out with the horses, Red and Sandy waited for sounds of shooting before cutting the telegraph wires. To do so earlier might prevent a routine message from going out. That would alert the Yankees, for cutting the wires was a regular habit of the Texas Light Cavalry when on patrol in Union territory.

On reaching the corner of the house, Dusty looked along its front. He saw nobody and kept moving. Once he had to creep on hands and knees beneath a window, with

Yankees officers talking inside the room, but he reached the big old white oak which—if Wexler's description had been correct—reared before the window of Trumpeter's office.

The gnarled condition of the trunk offered sufficient footholds for him to climb the twelve foot or so to the lowest branch. By keeping on the house's side of the trunk, he avoided detection by the main gate's sentries. Once in the branches, he moved fast. Nor did reaching the general's balcony prove difficult. Stepping from a branch on to the stone balustrade, he saw a chink of light glowing from the centre of the drawn drapes. That meant the room most likely had occupants. However its windows were open, relieving Dusty of the task of forcing an entry.

Advancing on silent feet, Dusty looked through the tiny gap in the drapes. Going by the single star on the epaulettes of the man standing by the desk, Dusty had found General Trumpeter's room. The other's actions caused him to wait instead of entering. Slipping a .32 calibre metal-case cartridge into the cylinder of a Smith & Wesson No. 2 Army revolver, Trumpeter pivoted its barrel down to connect with the frame. Even as Dusty prepared to step through the drapes, a knock at the door changed his plans. With an almost furtive, guilty air, Trumpeter cocked the revolver and placed it in the open right hand drawer of the desk. Dusty felt puzzled by what he saw. Surely a brigadier general, even if he was a soft-shell appointed for political rather than military reasons, ought to know better than leave a cocked revolver lying around.

"Come in," Trumpeter called, without closing the drawer.

A young lieutenant entered, the one-eighth of an inch gold cord down the outer seams of his trouser leg showing him to be a member of the staff. Behind him came a big, burly man wearing the double-breasted jacket and eagle-insignia of a colonel. Even without the buff facings of the uniform, different in shade to the normal cavalry yellow, Dusty recognized Colonel Verncombe of the 6th New Jersey Dragoons. He had seen the colonel from a distance on more than one occasion during the fighting at the Snake Ford.

"You can go, Mr. Frost," Trumpeter said and Dusty thought that he detected a signal pass between the general and lieutenant.

"What do you know about this?" Verncombe demanded, stalking to the desk as Frost backed from the room and closed the door.

Without looking at the sheet of paper thrown before him, Trumpeter scowled at his visitor and replied, "There's still a difference in our ranks, Verncombe!"

"To hell with rank!" Verncombe barked, tapping the paper with his right forefinger. "Did you put this damnable thing out?"

"What if I did?" challenged Trumpeter and sat down.

"It's monstrous, that's what. A general in the United States Army using his official position to settle a personal vendetta."

For a moment Trumpeter did not reply. His eyes flickered in the direction of the door and Dusty formed the conclusion that he expected somebody to arrive. Then the general swung his gaze back to Verncombe. In a casual-seeming gesture, Trumpeter inched his right hand towards the open drawer.

"Watch your words, Verncombe!" Trumpeter spat out. "Your conduct is mutinous—and not for the first time."

"If my conduct is mutinous, I'd like to know what you call your own," the colonel blazed back. "Having young Fog murdered by some stinking guerilla won't excuse your mistakes."

"Have a care, Verncombe!" Trumpeter snarled, speaking loud and darting another glance at the door. "You'll go too far!"

Suddenly everything became clear to Dusty. Now he understood why Trumpeter had loaded the revolver and placed it cocked in the open drawer. The exchange of signals between the general and Frost, taken with the interest in the door and over-loud comments gave the game away. Unless Dusty missed his guess, Trumpeter planned to kill

Verncombe and had done so before the other produced the damning bounty offer or spoke mutinously.

What was more, Dusty knew why. After so many failures Trumpeter must be under heavy fire from Washington and in danger of losing his command. So he planned to use an old method of worming out of difficulties. Select a scapegoat, someone who could be blamed for all the failures. And who better than the most senior colonel in the Army of Arkansas? Accuse Verncombe of everything— after he was dead and unable to refute the charges—and escape the consequences.

There might even be a more personal reason for selecting Verncombe. Whatever small credit accrued from the Snake Ford affair had gone to the colonel. Everybody knew—and Trumpeter knew that they knew—Verncombe had done well in straightening out his superior's muddles. So the general had every reason to hate the burly, competent Dragoon.

Dusty understood the whole situation; including that he must intervene or see the colonel murdered. From all appearances, Verncombe was too angry to see his danger and was headed for a carefully laid trap.

"Howdy," Dusty said, stepping quickly through the drapes and letting them fall back into place. If anybody outside had seen the flicker of light, they ought to be unaware of its cause. Or too uncertain to think it worth investigating.

"What the—?" Trumpeter gasped, staring goggle-eyed and jerking his hand from the drawer. Shocked by the sight of an armed Confederate cavalry officer in his office, he continued with almost inane gravity. "Who are you?"

Verncombe did not need to ask. Small the newcomer might be in feet and inches, but he gave the impression of far greater size. More than that, the colonel had seen Dusty during the brief Snake Ford campaign. A cold, sardonic grin twisted at Verncombe's lips; but he made no attempt to draw the revolver from his waistbelt holster despite Dusty's empty hands. Instead he turned his eyes to the general and performed the introduction with almost correct formality.

"General Trumpeter, meet Captain Dusty Fog."

"F-Fog!" Trumpeter repeated and could not prevent himself from asking, "What are you doing here?"

"I've come to make you call off those guerillas who got your bounty notes," Dusty replied.

Silence fell on the room, except for Trumpeter's laboured breathing. Sitting rigid in his chair, he stared as if mesmerised at the small Texan, without saying a word. It was left to Verncombe to break the silence. Even he needed a good thirty seconds to recover from finding himself in such an unbelievable situation. Through it all Dusty stood just inside the room. Legs slightly apart, he balanced on the balls of his feet and every fibre of his being stayed tuned ready for instant action. Having answered Trumpeter's question, he waited for the next move to be made.

"And if he won't?" Verncombe inquired at last.

"He'll do it, colonel," Dusty answered, sounding gentle as a summer breeze. Yet under the soft-spoken words lay a greater menace than could have come from the screamed-out threats of a lesser man. "He'll do it—or see if he can do better against me than Buller did."

There the Yankee officers had the whole matter laid before them as plainly as if the small Texan had spoken volumes in explanation. Either Trumpeter rescinded his offer of the reward, or he faced Dusty Fog with a gun in his hand. Still the general did not speak and once more Verncombe took up the conversation.

"You know about this letter then?"

"I know," Dusty agreed. "Because of it, a girl of seventeen was murdered."

"How do you mean?" Verncombe demanded.

"A guerilla had one of the letters and figured to collect the bounty. A cousin of mine, a young, pretty girl, colonel, got dressed in one of my uniforms and walked through Prescott wearing it for a joke— Only she didn't get all the way through. The guerilla saw her and, it was dark, figured he'd found me. He walked up and shot her."

"The hell you say!" Verncombe breathed and glared at Trumpeter.

The words broke Trumpeter's spell and he jerked himself upright in the chair. Up to then the shock of being confronted, in the supposed safety of his own residence, by the cause of his misfortunes had held him immobile. Seeing his subordinate's cold contemputous scowl jolted him back to reality. While aware of the peril, he also figured that it might help him out of his difficulties.

"Take him prisoner, Verncombe!" Trumpeter commanded.

"You put that bounty on him," the colonel replied, little realizing that he was approaching another trap. "I don't need the money, so do your own dirty work—if you've got the guts."

A flat refusal, or even any hesitation to obey, was what Trumpeter had hoped would happen. Now he had the excuse he wanted to kill—no, carry out a justifiable execution of Verncombe. It would merely be an extension of a plot hatched earlier that day. The major difference was that the colonel had come unbidden instead of being sent for.

Everything had been arranged before Frost had arrived to say that Colonel Verncombe wanted an interview. After leaving them together, the aide was to go to the Provost Marshal and say that he feared trouble from the "drunken" Verncombe. On reaching Trumpeter's office, they would hear voices raised in anger. Then, as they burst in with drawn guns, Trumpeter would take the Smith & Wesson from the drawer and shoot Verncombe dead. With a court martial threatened over his failure to keep Rose Greenhow a prisoner, the Provost Marshal would be inclined to accept any version of the incident given by his general.

Dusty Fog's presence would form only a slight impediment to the plan. He could not know of the revolver being so handy in the drawer. Anyway, he would be fully occupied with the two officers when they arrived. Possibly he would kill one of them, if the stories of how fast he could draw a gun were true. If so, Trumpeter hoped his aide would be the victim. Frost knew too much and would want more than a mere promotion to captain for his share in the

Dragoon colonel's death. Fast Fog might be, but one of the two was sure to get him while he shot the other.

First however, the stage must be set and the scene prepared.

"Take him, Verncombe!" the general bellowed, glancing at the door.

"Why don't you do it?" countered the Dragoon.

"Damn it, I'm not armed!"

No harm in fostering that illusion. A Texan, full of the idiotic chivalry of the South, would not fire on an unarmed man.

There it was!

The handle of the door turned slowly. Outside Frost and the Provost Marshal were waiting, guns drawn ready for use and the Texan still stood with empty hands.

"This is the last time, Verncombe!" Trumpeter shouted. "Take him. That is an order!"

As the door flung open and the two officers burst in, Trumpeter grabbed at the Smith & Wesson.

CHAPTER SEVENTEEN

He's Heading For the West Wall

Everything might have gone as Trumpeter hoped, but for three unforeseen circumstances.

First: Dusty expected Frost to return and figured that he would not come alone. He even guessed at the aide being accompanied by only one man. While Trumpeter wanted "proof" that he had acted within his rights, too many witnesses would be dangerous. One man, carefully selected, would tell a convincing story. The more involved, the greater the risk of confusion in their evidence.

Second: the small Texan knew about the hidden Smith & Wesson, so he was not fooled by the general's protestations of being unarmed.

Third: and most important: Trumpeter had no conception of the lightning speed and ambidextrous dexterity with which Dusty could handle his guns.

Rushing into the room with their revolvers held ready for use, Frost and the Provost Marshal found a different situation to that which they had expected. They skidded to a halt, staring at the small figure by the window. Quicker than Frost to recover his wits, the Provost Marshall started to move his gun around towards the officer wearing a uniform of Confederate grey.

Across flashed Dusty's hands, passing each other and working in perfect unison. The matched Colts swept from their holsters, angling outwards. Flame ripped from both barrels at almost the same moment; less than a second from when his hands began to move.

At the door, Frost saw Dusty partially disappear behind two swirling clouds of burned black powder's smoke from which sparked red spurts of flame. Just realizing the implications of what he saw, the aide felt a savage impact against his shoulder. Pain roared through him and he spun around, screaming, to fall into the passage beyond the door.

Still turning the barrel of his Colt, the Provost Marshal saw the same as Frost. A moment later he died. The bullet from Dusty's second Colt struck him between the eyes. In going backwards, he fired his revolver. Dusty felt the breeze of its lead passing his face.

Bringing the Smith & Wesson ready cocked from the drawer, Trumpeter started to point it in Verncombe's direction. Although he guessed the other's intentions, the colonel stood without a movement. Amazement twisted the satisfaction from Trumpeter's features as he saw his "rescuers" struck down by Dusty's bullets. Suddenly, shockingly, he realized that the small Texan had ruined another of his carefully-made plans. Fear, fury and self-preservation drove Trumpeter to react. Mouthing wild curses, he forgot Verncombe and tried to line the revolver on the greater danger.

Cocking his Colts, Dusty twisted his torso towards the desk. Like extensions of his will, the long barrels directed themselves to the Yankee general. First left then right hand revolver roared, coming so close together that the detonations barely formed two separate sounds. Trumpeter's head jolted as if struck by an invisible hand. The force of the two bullets' arrival lifted him backwards. Disintegrating under his weight, the chair on which he had fallen let him sprawl lifeless to the floor.

Again Dusty drew back the hammers of his guns, although he did so as an instinctive, trained reaction rather than by conscious thought. Turning, he brought the Colts in Verncombe's direction. The colonel stood with open hands dangling loosely at his sides, but Dusty knew it was not fear that kept him out of the fight. Career-soldier and man of honour, Verncombe could understand why Dusty had taken such a desperate chance. More than that, the colonel hated the deed which had caused the small Texan to come and face Trumpeter. As far as Verncombe was concerned, the War did not exist at that moment.

"Leave the letter," Verncombe said as shouts of alarm and running feet sounded in the passage.

"Sure, colonel," Dusty replied, lowering the hammers and twirling away the Colts. "Thanks."

With that the small Texan turned and stepped through the drapes. Two strides carried him across the balcony. His work in Little Rock was done. With Trumpeter dead, Verncombe would rescind the offer of a reward for Dusty's death. Now he must try to escape.

Down at the main gate, the two sentries faced the house, gesticulating and talking. If they had seen Dusty come through the drapes, they gave no sign of it. He stepped on to the balustrade and jumped into the tree. Landing on a branch, he climbed rapidly downwards. Just as he had hoped, all the activity was in the house. While men dashed to investigate the shooting, they stayed inside the building. That had been something Dusty had relied upon—or hoped would happen—when making his plans.

Who could blame the Yankees for not realizing what had happened? Nobody could have foreseen that a Rebel would dare break into the private residence of the general commanding the Union's Army of Arkansas.

Swinging from the lowest branch, Dusty dropped to the ground. He landed running, darting to the nearest of the decorative bushes and making for the east wall.

In Trumpeter's ofice, Verncombe had moved towards the end of the desk. He looked at the first of the men to enter the room and barked, "See if there's anything you can do for the general!"

Knowing that Trumpeter was beyond all human aid, the colonel sprang to the window. Passing through the drapes, he allowed them to fall back into place behind him. Striding along the balcony, he looked around. Drawing his revolver, he lined and fired it downwards.

"Over there!" he roared as the sentries ran towards the house. "He's heading for the *west* wall!"

Satisfied that he had diverted the search, for he guessed

which way Dusty had come into the grounds, Verncombe
returned to the window and blocked the other men's path as
they tried to emerge.

"Thanks again, colonel," Dusty breathed, continuing his
swift, crouching run through the garden.

Approaching the wall, he saw that its top had changed
shape. Two strange elongated humps lay on it. They stirred
as he drew nearer and Betty's voice came from one of
them.

"Jump, Dusty!"

Leaping up, Dusty felt his outstretched arms caught in
Betty's and Kiowa's hands. Aided by the girl's not inconsiderable strength, the power of the sergeant's wiry frame
took the strain of his captain's weight. Bracing his feet
against the wall, Dusty walked up it. From the top, Dusty
and his helpers dropped down to where Billy Jack was
discarding his borrowed disguise.

"Over there, *pronto!*" Dusty snapped.

Not until running towards the wall of the next building
did Dusty notice that his cousin had been thinking of herself. The skirt was gone, leaving her legs clad in riding
breeches and boots; which Dusty knew she had been wearing all the time. However, she had the unconscious sentry's
tunic on; its sleeves either rolled up or cut off to the desired
level. Dusty wondered which of them had realized that the
blouse's white material showed up in the dark and would
draw attention to its wearer.

The time was not suitable for Dusty to satisfy his curios-
ity. Already men from the adjacent house, disturbed by the
shooting and noise from the general's residence, were
coming to investigate. Fortunately they made so much
noise that it drowned out the sound of the Texans' running
feet. Flattening themselves against the wall of the building
nearest to the edge of town, Dusty's party watched soldiers
streaming by. The men went towards the front entrance of
Trumpeter's house, so missed seeing the four figures. Nor
did the rear wall's sentries do better, their attention being
concentrated on the inside of the grounds.

"Are you all right, Dusty?" Betty asked as they hurried away from the houses.

"Sure," he replied.

"How about Trumpeter?" Billy Jack inquired.

"He's dead," Dusty answered.

"Figured he might be," drawled the sergeant major. *"Now* we'll have another fire-eater coming out here looking to make life miserable for us."

"I thought you enjoyed being miserable," Betty pointed out.

"I do," Billy Jack confessed, then brightened up a little. "I never thought of it like that. Things ain't so bad after all."

"It's lucky that feller on the balcony got all twisted around like that," Kiowa remarked. "He sent them sentries off the wrong way."

"Real lucky," Dusty agreed.

The truth about Verncombe's "mistake" could ruin the colonel's career, so Dusty would never tell what had really happened.

Nobody saw them leave town. Behind them the alarm bell clanged, but they rejoined Red and Sandy, mounted their horses and rode south-east without hearing any sound of pursuit.

In Trumpeter's office, Verncombe looked at the assembled staff officers. All of the knew him and most of them respected him as a competent officer and good man.

"It was Dusty Fog," the colonel told them and picked up the sheet of paper. "He came as a result of this letter which the general had circulated amongst the guerilla bands."

While the letter passed from hand to hand, accompanied by startled or angry exclamations at its contents, Verncombe explained how it had been the cause of Georgina Blaze's death.

Sitting on a chair in the corner of the office, having his shoulder bandaged, Frost watched and listened. It quickly became obvious that the senior officers present, the ones whose opinions counted in the final analysis, felt revulsion at the letter and disagreed with its purpose. Sick with pain and anxiety, he gave thought to saving his own skin. Deciding that his only hope lay in transferring the blame, he sought for a way of doing it.*

By the time the note had been read, the officer-of-the-day and sergeant-of-the-guard arrived to report that the search of the grounds had been without result. The officer was under the impression that the intruder had gone to the west, then doubled back behind the house to go over the east-side wall. The sentry from that section had been found, stripped of his overcoat and tunic, bound and gagged, against one of the adjacent buildings.

While that information was being digested, a breathless soldier dashed in to say that every telegraph wire out of town had been cut. Wexler had supplied men to help with that part of Dusty's plan.

"That's Fog's way all right," growled the Quartermaster's Department colonel, bitterly aware that he would have to produce wire to replace the missing lengths. Like all members of his Department, he hated parting with any kind of stores.

"Orders, sir?" prompted the Town Major, looking at the senior officer present—and, with Trumpeter dead, acting commanding general of the Army of Arkansas.

"First we must rescind this bounty offer," Verncombe stated firmly. "I want that starting *now*, without any delay, and completed as quickly as possible."

Mutters of agreement followed the words. None of the older officers wanted it even thought that members of the United States Army condoned Trumpeter's behaviour in

---

*Frost later declared that Trumpeter and the Provost Marshal had conspired to murder Verncombe, but insisted that he had been an innocent pawn and had intended to warn the colonel. While nobody believed his story, it could not be disproved and it came in useful as a means of avoiding a too-close examination of Verncombe's conduct after the shooting. Wishing to disassociate themselves from Trumpeter's actions, the Union's high command were anxious for the affair to pass over without complications.

placing the bounty. So they saw the urgency to make a public retraction.

"Next we'll organize a search of the town" Verncombe went on. "I want patrols ready to leave at dawn. They'd never pick up Fog's trail in the dark."

"It will give him a good start over our men," the officer of the day protested. "We should alert the garrisons between here and the Ouachita River so that they can get out searching parties."

"That's true enough," agreed the Town Major, an infantry officer with no clear idea of the difficulties involved in doing so.

Thinking of the superb riding skill and excellent horses of the Texas Light Cavalry, Verncombe doubted if any man in his command could reach the garrison before Dusty Fog and his party were safely by them.

"Select your best courier, major," the colonel ordered. "Send him off as quickly as you can." He raised his eye piously towards the roof and continued, "I sure *hope* he gets there in time."

WANTED:
Hard Drivin' Westerns From

J.T. Edson